The Happy Hollisters

and the

Cowboy Mystery

BY JERRY WEST

Illustrated by Helen S. Hamilton

THE SVENSON GROUP, INC.
on behalf of The Hollister Family Properties Trust

Jacket copy from the original hardcover book:

"Domingo," the burro the Hollisters were given for a pet the last time they were out West, is the innocent means by which the Hollisters once again find themselves following the mystery trail on horseback.

Because of a near accident the Hollister children meet and befriend the Blairs, who are from Nevada. They learn that Mr. Blair is trying to sell some of his property on the Tumbling K Ranch, but strange and eerie events have discouraged prospective buyers. Naturally, the minute the Hollisters hear mystery is involved they are eager to be in the thick of it. Their interest is further aroused when a prowler is discovered spying on them in Shoreham. What excitement there is then, when they are invited to visit the Blairs and help them solve this baffling problem.

Who is the strange and evil looking man who tries to cause trouble for the Hollisters on their trip to Nevada? And who is the tall, lanky cowboy, Dakota Dawson, whose actions are so suspicious? And are the strange lights seen on the mountain man-made or some odd trick of nature?

The Happy Hollisters find fun, adventure, danger, and the answers to the many questions posed by the mystery surrounding the Tumbling K Ranch.

ISBN: 1978384513

ISBN-13: 9781978384514

Dedication

The Happy Hollisters and the Cowboy Mystery is Volume 20 in a 33-book series. The books are being reissued in honor of my grandfather, Andrew Edward Svenson, who began *The Happy Hollisters* series in 1953 using the pseudonym Jerry West. The characters in the Hollister family were based in part on his family – my grandmother, father, uncle, and aunts – and I am grateful to them for inspiring these books, and for their support of this labor of love:

Marian S. Svenson – "Elaine Hollister"
Andrew E. Svenson, Jr. – "Pete"
Laura Svenson Schnell – "Pam"
Eric R. Svenson, Sr. – "Ricky"
Jane Svenson Kossmann – "Holly"
Eileen Svenson de Zayas and Ingrid Svenson Herdman – "Sue"

Many thanks also to Callie and Libby Svenson
for their editorial and marketing assistance.

Andrew E. Svenson III
The Svenson Group, Inc.
on behalf of The Hollister Family Properties Trust

*"Friends of the children are friends of ours. And since we have five
children, we have lots of friends!"*

Contents

CHAPTER 1

Western Friends

RICKY Hollister leaned forward to speak into the burro's twitching ears. "Domingo," he said, "hold still. How else can Pam and I see the license plates?"

"Eee-aw!" brayed Domingo.

Pam, seated on the pet behind her brother, laughed at the little donkey's reply. Then she said quickly, "There goes Wisconsin!"

Pam and Ricky had ridden Domingo to the side of the main highway on the outskirts of Shoreham. They were counting out-of-state cars that whizzed past.

Ricky was seven. He had red hair and freckles on his impish nose. Pam, who was ten, had fluffy golden hair and brown eyes, which were fixed on the next car speeding toward them.

Just then Domingo decided to cross the road.

"Hey, stop!" Ricky cried out in alarm.

Pam was speechless with fright as Domingo took three more steps and halted in the middle of the highway.

The children slapped the sides of the burro, but he did not budge. The oncoming car slowed down a bit; then, with screeching brakes, it swerved to the side of the road. There was a loud bang as it slowed to a stop.

The car doors swung open. From the driver's seat stepped a tall, good-looking man. As he ran toward the burro, two children got out the other side and stood by the road.

The man gave Domingo a shove. "Get along with you!" he shouted, and the burro obediently crossed the road.

As the Hollisters slid to the ground, Pam noticed another car driving slowly past. From the corner of her eye she recognized a Colorado license plate, but her attention was quickly drawn to the man who had saved them. Now for the first time she realized he was dressed in Western togs, as were the two children.

"Oh, thank you!" Pam said. "You saved our lives."

"Burros are unpredictable," the man replied, smiling. "By the way, I'm Ken Blair, and these are my children, Bunky and Gina."

The boy was twelve, slender and wiry with black hair and a sunburned face. Gina, Pam guessed, was about eleven. Like her brother, she wore blue jeans, a colorful shirt, and wide-brimmed cowboy hat. Gina had brown bobbed hair and smiling blue eyes.

Pam and Ricky introduced themselves. "We live here in Shoreham," Pam added, pointing to the direction of their house, which was located on the edge of Pine Lake.

"We're from Nevada," Gina said. "We live on the Tumbling K Ranch near Elkton."

Mr. Blair added that they had been to New York and were on their way home. "I'm glad my car has good brakes," he said with a chuckle, then pointed to the right rear tire, which was flat. "I must have hit a sharp stone on a shoulder of the road."

"We heard the blowout," Ricky said. "I'm sorry about that, too, Mr. Blair. But I'll help you change the tire."

While the rancher, Ricky, and Bunky started to jack up the car and remove the wheel, Gina stroked Domingo's neck and chatted with Pam.

"We had an adventure in the Southwest once," Pam said, "but we've never been to Nevada."

"Oh, you'd like it," Gina replied. "Our ranch is at the foot of the Ruby Mountains."

"We love our home here, too," Pam said. "Would you like to see it, Gina?"

The girl turned to her father. "Daddy, may I go to Pam's house while you change the tire?"

"All right, dear, if it's not too far."

"It isn't," Pam assured him, and the two girls climbed onto Domingo's back. As they jogged across a field toward the lake front, Pam asked Gina, "Were you sightseeing in New York?"

"Not exactly. We went to New York because of a mystery."

"Oh, we love mysteries!" Pam exclaimed. "Is your mystery a big secret?"

"I think I can tell you," Gina replied. But before she had a chance to say more, two boys ran across the field toward them.

"Are they friends of yours?" the Nevada girl asked.

"Not exactly," Pam said. She told Gina that the taller boy was Joey Brill. He was twelve and large for his age, and Gina could already see that he wore a scowl on his face. The other boy was Will Wilson, who usually joined Joey in playing mean tricks.

"Pam, wait for us!" Joey called out as he and Will raced up to them.

"What do you want, Joey?" Pam asked.

"A ride on Domingo!"

"Not now. I'm taking Gina to our house."

"Ha ha!" Will laughed. "Where did you find that phony cowgirl? She doesn't live around here."

"Don't be so rude!" Pam said. "Gina lives on a ranch in Nevada."

"That means she's used to walking," Joey said. Without a word of warning, he grabbed Pam's arm and pulled her off the burro's back. At the same time Will pushed Gina off the other side.

As the girls protested, the two bullies hopped on the donkey. Will sat facing forward, Joey facing backward. Will yelled, "Giddap, Domingo."

Frightened, Domingo trotted off, with Pam and Gina running along behind him.

"Stop! Give back my burro!" Pam cried out.

Her excited voice carried to the highway. Ricky looked up and realized what had happened.

"Excuse me," he said quickly. "I've got to take care of those bullies!"

"Two against one isn't fair," said Bunky. "Let me help you."

"Sure, come on!"

"No fisticuffs, Bunky," Mr. Blair ordered.

"Okay, Dad."

Before setting off with Ricky, Bunky reached into the back seat of the car and pulled out a long rope.

"A lasso!" Ricky exclaimed.

"I always keep one handy," Bunky said, as the two boys ran toward the burro.

Fortunately, at this moment Domingo had another one of his balky spells, which gave Ricky and Bunky a chance to catch up with him.

"Make them get off Domingo," Pam called out as the two boys approached.

"Think you're big enough?" Joey Brill scowled.

Bunky did not reply, but made a loop in his lariat. As he swung it over his head, the loop became larger and larger.

"Out West we call this a Mother Hubbard loop," said Bunky. "An extra big one!"

Seeing what was coming, Joey and Will kicked Domingo, and the donkey started off again. Bunky tossed the lasso. It sailed through the air, landing neatly over the two boys.

Then Bunky pulled the rope tight, binding the riders together like Siamese twins.

"Let go!" Joey cried furiously.

As Domingo plodded on, Joey and Will were pulled off the burro's back. Joey hit the ground first, and Will landed on top of him.

"Oof!" Joey cried.

"Ow! My nose!" Will moaned.

The bullies struggled free of the loop and scrambled angrily to their feet. But the fight had been knocked out of them.

Bunky pulled the rope tight.

Both boys retreated, Joey shaking his fist at Bunky and shouting, "I'll get even with you for this! And with the rest of the Hollisters too!"

As soon as he and Will were out of sight, Pam and Ricky thanked the young cowboy.

"Yikes!" said Ricky. "You really know how to use a rope, Bunky."

"Old Dad taught me," he replied.

"But your father isn't old," Pam protested.

Bunky and Gina both laughed and explained that Old Dad Callahan was a cowboy who worked on the Tumbling K Ranch.

"You'd love him," Gina added.

Just then Mr. Blair called from the highway, saying that he was ready to go.

"But you haven't seen our home yet," Pam said sadly. "Could you and your father stop by?"

"I'll ask him," Gina promised, and with Bunky ran back to the car. Ricky tagged along.

"All right, if you children wish," Mr. Blair said, wiping his hands on a piece of cloth. "Perhaps we can wash up there, too."

Ricky hopped into the car and directed the travelers to the Hollister home, while Pam rode Domingo. Because Pam took a short cut, she arrived a few seconds ahead of the Nevada car, and led Domingo into his stall in the garage next to the house.

"Hornytoads!" Bunky exclaimed when the car entered the pebbly driveway. "What a dandy place!"

They got out and looked at the rambling three-story house. It had green lawns all around, shaded in spots by lovely trees. The back of the property bordered the lake.

"It's a beauty," Mr. Blair remarked. "We could use that water in Nevada—driest state in the Union."

Pam ran ahead to tell her parents about the callers. Mr. Hollister, a tall, athletic-looking man, was reading the newspaper in the living room. His wife, a pretty blond-haired woman, was in the kitchen, preparing supper.

"This is most unusual," Mr. Blair said with a boyish grin, as introductions were made. "We're perfect strangers and have no right to drop in."

"There are no strangers in our home," Mr. Hollister said, offering his hand. His brown eyes crinkled at the corners, and he added, "Friends of the children are friends of ours. And since we have five children, we have lots of friends!"

"Yes indeed. We're glad to see you," Mrs. Hollister said, coming in from the kitchen and removing her apron. "This is our oldest son, Pete."

The good-looking boy of twelve, with a crew cut and sparkling blue eyes, stepped forward to shake hands. Holly was introduced next. Twirling one of her brown pigtails, the six-year-old giggled and said hello.

Just then Sue Hollister, who was four, burst into the room, followed by Zip, their collie. Sue had black bobbed hair and chubby legs. Seeing the newcomers, she dashed into her father's arms.

"Daddy," she whispered, "I want a cowgirl hat like that."

In a few moments Sue had lost her shyness and took Gina by the hand. "Would you like to see my dolls?" she asked. "They're upstairs in my room."

"Oh, yes, please show me!"

The three Hollister girls led Gina up the carpeted steps, while the boys remained in the living room with their fathers.

"Hollister—Hollister," Mr. Blair said thoughtfully. "When I played football in college there was a fellow by that name on the State team."

Mr. Hollister leaned forward eagerly in his chair. "I'm the one!" he exclaimed.

"You played halfback?"

"Sure."

"And caught the winning touchdown pass the year State was champion?"

"Correct!"

"I was the left guard on my team," Mr. Blair said. "That was a hard game to lose, John."

Ricky, Pete, and Bunky listened with mouths agape. Both of their dads had been football heroes. How they wished that they could be the same some day!

"Crickets, Dad!" Pete exclaimed. "Tell us about that touchdown play!"

Mr. Hollister rose, walked over to the sofa, and picked up a small pillow. "Maybe I can show you better," he said. "Come on, Ken. Let's give these boys a demonstration."

He handed Ricky the cushion. "You be the center," he said.

"And I'll be the center on Dad's team," Bunky replied, facing Ricky in the middle of the living room rug.

"This is going to be fun," Ken Blair remarked.

Ricky tossed the pillow between his legs to his father. It flew to one side.

"Hey, Dad! Look out!" Pete cried as Mr. Hollister lunged into a lamp on an end table. He caught the pillow, but the lamp teetered toward the floor. Bunky Blair made a dive for it!

CHAPTER 2

A Faraway Puzzle

BUNKY caught the lamp in his arms a moment before it would have crashed to the floor. •

"Great play!" Pete said. "You saved the day that time, Bunky."

Mr. Hollister had a rueful expression when his wife entered the room in time to see Bunky replace the lamp on the table.

"I was just demonstrating some football to the boys," Mr. Hollister said as he fluffed the pillow and replaced it on the sofa. At that moment the girls trooped down the stairs, and Mr. Blair rose to say good-by.

"Gracious!" Mrs. Hollister protested. "You can't leave now. I've prepared enough food for all of us."

"But—but—" Mr. Blair began.

"No buts about it," Mr. Hollister said. "You're an old friend."

"Of course," Pete added. "You went to different colleges together!"

"Well, all right, and thank you," the Westerner said, making a helpless gesture. "I call this real eastern hospitality."

While they were eating dinner, Mr. Blair explained the reason for their trip to New York. "I'm trying to sell a part of our ranch," he said, "because it has proved to be unprofitable for raising cattle."

"That's too bad," Pam remarked sympathetically.

"Does your buyer live in New York?" Pete asked.

Mr. Blair said "Yes." A businessman named Simpson was about to purchase a piece of land, but he backed out of the deal because his daughter, Millie, was a fearful child.

"What's she afraid of?" Holly asked.

"Of one of the mysteries," Bunky replied. "Millie's afraid of lights that have been seen on our mountaintop after dark."

"I guess it is a little spooky," Gina spoke up. "So far as we know there's nobody on the mountain."

Mr. Blair went on to explain that Millie and her mother were spending the summer at a hotel in Elkton and that Millie took riding lessons at the Tumbling K.

"I don't think you'd like her," Bunky said, wrinkling his nose.

"But I bet we could solve the mystery!" Ricky declared.

"We're a detective family," Holly added.

"Hush, children," their mother said. "The Blairs will think you're bragging."

Pam smiled. "I don't say we can solve every mystery, Mr. Blair, but we did solve the mystery at Missile Town." Pam told briefly about their visit to Florida and how they had found the missing nose cone of a giant rocket.

"Then maybe you can solve our mystery, too!" Gina said eagerly.

"That would be excellent," Mr. Blair agreed. "How about your coming to visit us at the Tumbling K?"

Holly, who was helping her mother serve dessert, became so excited that she nearly dropped a piece of apple pie in Pete's lap. "Oh, goody!" she exclaimed. "We can ride horses and climb the mountain—and—"

Just then Gina glanced out the window. A startled expression came over her face and she cried out, "An Indian! I saw an Indian!"

Chairs were pushed back in haste, and all rushed out to investigate. As Pete raced around the side of the house he nearly bumped into a short, muscular, brown-skinned man.

"Indy Roades!" Pete cried. "What are you doing here?"

"I came to see your dad on some business," he replied as the others gathered around.

"That's the man I saw!" Gina declared breathlessly.

"He won't hurt you," Mr. Hollister said with a smile. "Indy's an old friend and a trusted employee."

Mr. Hollister went on to say that Indy was an honest-to-goodness Southwest Indian, who worked at the Trading Post, a combination hardware, toy, and sports shop which Mr. Hollister operated in downtown Shoreham.

After introducing his helper to the Blairs, Mr. Hollister asked, "Why were you looking in the window, Indy?"

"I saw a prowler," came the reply. "A man was hiding in the bushes there. As I frightened him away, I took a quick look in the window to see what he was peering at. Then I chased him to the road."

Indy said that the eavesdropper jumped into a car with an out-of-state license plate and made a speedy getaway. "He was a small man," the Indian added, "with close-cropped blond hair."

When Indy described the car, Pam gasped. "That sounds like the one with the Colorado license plates that passed us after you got the flat tire, Mr. Blair!"

"Hornytoads!" Bunky exclaimed. "I wonder if he's the same one who was following us in New York!"

Before Bunky had time to explain further, Pete ran into the house and telephoned Officer Cal Newberry. He was a young, handsome Shoreham policeman who often helped the Hollisters solve their mysteries. When he heard the story, Officer Cal promised to check on the Hollister property from time to time during the night.

After Indy left, the others returned to the house to finish their dessert. While they ate, Bunky told more of the mystery which had followed them all the way to New York.

"Bunky's right," Mr. Blair said. "We were being followed in New York, but I don't know why." He told them, for example, that the car behind his in Central Park had tried to squeeze him off the winding road.

"And we almost hit a stone underpass," Bunky said.

"I think several people were following us," Gina added.

"Maybe a gang is after you," Ricky suggested, his eyes widening with excitement.

"Well, you'll be safe here for the night," Mrs. Hollister said with a smile at Gina and Bunky.

The Western children grinned. "Are we going to stay here really?" Bunky asked.

"We shouldn't impose on your hospitality," their father protested.

"We love having you," Mrs. Hollister assured him as they rose from the table. "It's much too late for you to find a motel now."

Pete and Bunky then carried in the suitcases, and Mrs. Hollister and Pam showed the guests their rooms on the third floor. As they came down into the living room again, Gina said, "Daddy, may we tell about the other mystery, too?"

"Another one!" Pete exclaimed. "Crickets! Nevada must be a mysterious state!"

"We do have another riddle to solve," Mr. Blair said. "Some men are stealing baby antelopes in the valley near our ranch."

"It's against the law," Bunky announced sternly.

"Oh, that's too bad," little Sue said. "What are antelopes?"

When she was told they were something like deer, Sue looked sad. "Oh, those bad men!" she declared, stamping her foot. "We'll catch them too!"

"They're pretty slippery characters," the rancher said. "After they snare the little antelopes, the men seem to vanish into thin air."

"We have some babies, too," Holly put in, beckoning to Gina and Bunky. "Come on, I'll show you."

The pigtailed girl led the way down the cellar steps and pointed to a large box lined with rags. Inside sat White Nose, their pet cat, who was all black except for her nose. She was a mother cat and around her were snuggled her five kittens.

"You have a herd of cattle," Holly said impishly, "and we have a herd of cats."

"A litter, silly," corrected Pam, and she bent down to pick up White Nose. Pete scooped up two kittens and handed one to Bunky to hold.

"Oh, they're darling!" Gina said. "What are their names?"

"Midnight, Snowball, Smoky, Tutti-Frutti, and Cuddly," Sue explained, ticking them off on her chubby fingers.

"Let's play roundup time with the kittens," Gina suggested. She picked up a piece of string from a nearby table, fashioned a small loop, and tried to drop it over the head of Snowball.

But the kitten did not like this idea. She jumped out of the box, ran across the cellar floor, and jumped up one step at a time, finally disappearing into the kitchen.

"Snowball, come here!" Holly cried. "Don't run away from our company. It isn't polite."

Holly ran up from the cellar, followed by the others. They looked all about the first floor but could find no sign of the white kitten.

"I'm sorry I frightened her," Gina said. "Do you suppose she ran away from home?"

The kitten did not like to play roundup time.

"Don't worry," Pam said. "Let's look upstairs."

The children searched all their bedrooms on the second floor, but Snowball was not there. Then they climbed to the third floor, where the Blairs were to spend the night.

"I see her!" Gina cried finally. "Look here!"

The kitten was snuggled down inside Gina's cowgirl hat, which lay at the foot of her bed.

"See, Snowball likes you after all, Gina," declared Sue with a giggle.

"May she sleep here tonight?" asked Gina, picking up Snowball and stroking her.

"Of course, if you'd like her to," Pam said.

Just then Mrs. Hollister called up from the living room, "Children—time for bed!"

Regretfully the Hollisters said goodnight to their guests and started down to their rooms. "First I'll tie Zip outside, just in case any more prowlers come around," Pete said. A short time afterward, he was in bed.

The night passed without alarm. When Pam awoke next morning and peeked into Sue's room, she noticed that her little sister was not there. Shortly afterward the fragrant aroma of pancakes announced that breakfast was nearly ready. But Sue had not appeared even by the time the Blairs were seated at the table.

"Where can that child be?" Mrs. Hollister asked.

"She's probably playing by the lake," Pete said. "I'll call her, Mother."

Before Pete could rise from his chair, the door banged and Sue scampered into the dining room. "Ha ha, look at me!" she called out.

"Gracious!" Mrs. Hollister exclaimed. "Sue, what have you done to your hair?"

To the amazement of everybody, Sue had a blond crew cut!

CHAPTER 3

Piggy-bank Raiders

"Guess what I did to my hair!" Sue Hollister cried gleefully.

As the little girl skipped into the dining room, Pam shut her eyes. "Oh no!" she said. "You didn't cut your hair!"

"She must have bleached it, too," Ricky said. To himself he thought, "A neat trick!" and he looked fondly at his sister.

"Ha ha, I fooled you," declared Sue. "I'm wearing a wig."

She pulled it from her head. When Mrs. Hollister saw the black bobbed hair again, she sighed with relief.

"You little rascal," Pete said. "You had us all foxed that time."

"Where did you get it?" Pam asked.

"I found it," Sue replied breezily, and handed the wig to Ricky to try on.

"Where?" Pete asked.

"Out by the curb." Sue helped herself to some flapjacks and poured maple syrup over them, just as if finding wigs was something that happened every day.

"But, Sue!" Pete continued. "This is important. Exactly at what spot?"

The little girl chewed a luscious bite for a moment before replying. "Right next to the driveway."

The Blairs had looked on in silent wonder until Bunky exclaimed, "Hornytoads!" He snapped his fingers. "Maybe that wig is a clue!"

"Just what I was thinking," said Pete. "Mother, as soon as we've finished, will you please excuse us?"

"Of course, dear."

A few moments later, he pushed back his chair and beckoned to Pam, Bunky, and Gina. Soon the four children were in front of the house, searching the spot where Sue had found the wig.

"I'll bet it was dropped by the man who was spying on us," Pete said.

Pam agreed. "Maybe only one person was following you in New York," she told the Blair children. "He might have been wearing various disguises."

Gina did not agree entirely. "One of the persons was a woman," she objected. "Do you think a man would wear dresses?"

Pete shrugged and replied, "It's possible. But I wouldn't like to do it."

The Hollisters thought it would be wise to turn the wig over to Officer Cal for his investigation. Pete telephoned the young police officer, who arrived in the squad car a few minutes later.

"This might be a good clue, Pete," he said, taking the crew-cut wig. "But the chances are that prowler is miles away by now."

As for the wig itself, Officer Cal said he would try to trace it to the place where it was sold, but he thought this would take a lot of time.

The Blairs, meanwhile, prepared to leave the Hollister home and continue their trip to Nevada. After the breakfast dishes were cleared, Pam and Holly helped their mother pack a picnic lunch for their visitors.

Holly spread butter on pieces of bread, and her mother made the sandwiches. Then Pam wrapped them in wax paper and put the food in a small carton. Mrs. Hollister included fruit, a can of juice, and paper cups. She presented the lunch to the Blairs after they were packed and seated in their car.

"Thank you so much, Mrs. Hollister," Gina said.

"I just can't wait until lunch time," Bunky added, grinning.

"Now don't forget," Mr. Blair said before he pulled out of the driveway, "we want you to visit us and solve the mysteries."

Both Mr. and Mrs. Hollister, as well as the children, thanked the Westerners for their kind invitation.

"We can't say for sure whether we'll come or not," Mr. Hollister said.

"I do hope we meet again some day," Pam said wistfully.

"Of course we will," Gina said, and leaned out the window to give Mrs. Hollister a surprise kiss on the cheek.

"Good-by! Good-by!" everyone called. The Nevada car drove off and disappeared down the street as they all waved.

"Yikes!" Ricky said sadly. "I hate to see them go. We had so much fun and mystery while they were here."

As Mr. Hollister departed for the Trading Post a few minutes later, he reminded Pete and Ricky that they had grass to cut. The boys went straight to the garage for the mower and clippers.

Pam and Holly climbed to the third floor to tidy the guest rooms. Sue tagged along behind them, carrying Smoky, the kitten, under her right arm like a purse.

As Pam stretched a fresh sheet on one of the beds and tucked it in, she said, "Holly, I have an idea."

"I know what," Holly teased. "You want to write Bunky a letter."

"No, silly," Pam said, "not that." Then she went on as she plumped the pillows into place. "If we do go out West, wouldn't it be nice to buy Mother a new wallet for her driver's license?"

"That would be keen!" Holly agreed as she helped Pam smooth the counterpane.

"Do you have money enough?" Sue asked. She sat on a chair, swinging her legs and stroking the kitten.

"I have some money in my piggy bank," Pam said.

"Me too," said Holly.

"Then let's do it right away," suggested Sue. She set the kitten on the floor, and Smoky, holding her tail as straight as a flagpole, hastened to rejoin White Nose in the basement.

The girls hurried to their bedrooms, where each of them kept her piggy bank on the dresser. Sue's pig was a small white one with red polka dots. Holly's pig was twice the size, with a broad snout. The bank that Pam

They shook the pennies and silver out of their banks.

took from her dresser and placed on the bed was a blue one decorated with tiny rosebuds. As she started to empty the coins, her two sisters ran into the room. They stood beside the bed, shaking the pennies and silver out of their banks. When the clickety-click of the coins had ceased, the bedspread was covered with money. Pam counted it quickly.

"It's six dollars and fifty-nine cents," Pam reported, as she scooped the money up into a small pile.

"We should be able to buy a dandy wallet with that much," Holly declared.

Sue found a small brown paper bag and Pam put the money in it. Then the sisters hurried downstairs and out the front door.

When Ricky saw them headed toward the street, he shut off the noisy power mower and asked, "Where are you going in such a hurry?"

"It's a secret," Holly answered, wrinkling her freckled nose.

"Then I'll go with you!"

"Not so fast," said Pete. He was on his haunches, clipping the grass bordering the driveway. "We have to finish our job, Ricky," he added.

Ricky eyed the brown bag and asked what was in it, but Pam would not tell him. Then the red-haired boy started the lawn mower again and raced back and forth over the green grass. He hoped to finish in time to follow his sisters and find out what the secret was about.

Pam, Holly, and Sue, holding hands, walked quickly along the tree-shaded sidewalk toward the Shoreham shopping center. When they were halfway there, Joey

Brill appeared around the corner of a side street and hailed them. "Where are your friends with the funny clothes?" he asked, running up to Pam.

"They've left," she replied, continuing on her way.

Joey strode along beside her. "I was going to get even with you for pulling me off Domingo," he said. "But I'll forget it if you give me some of that candy."

"What candy?" Pam asked.

"In the brown bag."

"It isn't candy," Holly declared. "It's—"

Pam gave her sister a nudge, which silenced the pig-tailed girl.

"If it isn't candy, then what is it?"

Pam ignored the bully. She walked even faster, holding Sue by one hand, and glancing up and down the street for someone who might come to her aid. But there was no one in sight.

"All right," Joey said. "If you won't show me what's in that bag I'll—*take it!*"

He snatched the sack from Pam's hand and raced across the street with it.

"Stop, you old meanie!" Pam cried out, and ran after him.

Just then Pete and Ricky appeared far down the street riding their bicycles. Seeing what had happened, the two boys stood up on the pedals and pumped furiously. They quickly caught up to Joey, racing along the sidewalk.

Pete leaped off his bicycle and sprinted after him. The bully zigzagged to elude Pete, and finally dashed across the street. Pete caught up with him in the center of the road, leaped on his back, and bore Joey to the pavement. As he did, the paper bag broke open, scattering coins all over the street.

Pete and Joey tussled, rolling over and over. Pete was on the bottom when they reached the curb, and his head hit the hard edge of the cement.

"Ow!" he cried. Stunned for the moment, Pete released his grip on Joey. The larger boy sprang to his feet and raced on down the street. He soon outdistanced Ricky.

Pete, meanwhile, rose and gingerly felt the large egg rising on the back of his head.

"Crickets!" he said with a half grin. "I saw stars!"

"And you saved our money!" Holly cried. "Hurry, we must pick it up."

Ricky trotted back and joined Pete, Pam, Sue, and Holly in retrieving the pennies, nickels, dimes, and quarters which had rolled over the pavement in all directions. Just then several cars came along, and Ricky manfully held up his hand like a traffic policeman to stop them while Pete and the girls picked up the last few coins.

"All right, proceed slowly," Ricky said. He whistled and motioned the cars to continue.

"I'd make a pretty good traffic cop, don't you think?" Ricky asked as Pam sat on the curb and carefully counted the money.

It was all there except a nickel. Pete reached into his pocket and pulled out a five-cent piece. "Here, this will make up for the one you lost," he said.

"Will you tell us what the secret is now?" Ricky asked.

"All right," said Pam, "but don't tell Mother. It's a surprise for her." After being informed of the girls' plan, the boys grinned happily and agreed that it was a good idea. Then Pam knotted the money in her handkerchief. The two boys escorted the girls to the shopping center on their bikes and then rode back to the house.

When Mr. Hollister arrived home that evening, he praised Pete and Ricky for their good job of grass cutting. As he stood at the window, admiring the well-trimmed lawns, Pam called everyone to supper.

Toward the end of the meal, Pam nodded to Holly and Holly nudged Sue. The little girl rose from her chair and placed a small package before her mother.

"Gracious, what's this?" Mrs. Hollister asked.

"It's a present," Holly replied.

"Something you'll need for our trip out West," Pam added. "Open it."

"Oh dear, I don't like to disappoint you children," Mrs. Hollister said, "but we may not go to Nevada."

"Well, just in case we do," Holly said, "you'll need this."

Their mother opened the package and gasped in surprise when she saw the beautiful black leather wallet. On it were the initials EH for Elaine Hollister.

"What beautiful silver work!" Mrs. Hollister said, admiring the letters. "And I love the wallet. So many places for pictures of you children!" She rose and kissed them all, and as she did the telephone rang. Pete hastened to answer it.

"Hello?" Pete listened. "Oh, Mr. Blair. Sure, I'll let you speak to Dad."

Pete held the phone toward his father.

"Hello, Ken," John Hollister began, and continued the conversation for several minutes. He hung up, shaking his head, and returned smiling to the table.

"Don't keep us in suspense, Daddy," Pam said. "What did Mr. Blair say?"

"He insists that we visit the Tumbling K," Mr. Hollister replied. He said that the rancher had telephoned his home and learned that the mysterious situation had become worse during the past few days.

"More mysterious lights, more antelopes stolen," Mr. Hollister said.

"Then we can go, can't we, Daddy?" Ricky asked, scrambling to his father's side and putting an arm around his shoulder.

"I'm really too busy at the store."

"Then Mother can take us," Pete said with a chuckle. "And she can use her new wallet!"

The discussion bounced back and forth, gathering more enthusiasm with each plea by the five Hollister children.

"It really is a grand opportunity," Mrs. Hollister declared finally. "Suppose I drive the children out there, John."

"Yippee! Hurray for Mother!" Holly shouted.

"I'm sure you can manage it," Mr. Hollister told her after the gleeful cries had died down.

"It will take a day or two to get ready," Mrs. Hollister said. "Meanwhile we can send a telegram to the Blairs saying we're coming."

Pam and her mother busied themselves the next day getting things ready for the long trip. Sue watched happily as they checked over the clothes the children would need. Pete went to the Trading Post to help his father. Ricky and Holly, meanwhile, sat on their dock at the lake's edge.

"I just can't wait to see Nevada," Ricky said.

"Why don't we play Tumbling K Ranch right now while we're waiting?" his sister suggested. Just then they heard some splashing in the water nearby and turned to see Joey Brill approaching in his canoe.

"Stay away from here," Ricky warned, "or I'll call Pete!"

"Let's be friends," Joey said, "and play a game."

"We were going to play Tumbling K Ranch," Holly said. "That's where we're going out West."

"Sounds great," Joey replied. He tied the canoe and scrambled onto the dock. "Tell me more about it."

Joey listened very politely while Ricky and Holly revealed their plans. "I bet I know somebody who'd like to know all this," he said teasingly. "And I know just where I can find him."

"Who do you mean?" Ricky asked.

"A man," Joey replied. "He stopped me on the street after we had that fight yesterday and asked me all about you."

"Why?" Holly asked eagerly. "What did he want?"

"Yikes! Maybe it was the prowler again," Ricky explained, his eyes big with excitement.

"Ha-ha-ha!" Joey laughed. "Don't get scared. I was only fooling."

Ricky and Holly exchanged looks. "You were only making it up?" the girl asked Joey doubtfully.

"Sure," he said, but he didn't look her in the eye. "Come on," he coaxed. "Let's play Tumbling K."

"But we haven't any cattle—not even any antelopes," Ricky said.

"Mr. Johnson the farmer has some," Joey told him. "Come on. Hop in my canoe and I'll take you there. It's just around the bend of the lake."

"Oh, no, we won't," Holly said. "We'll go there on our bikes and you can meet us."

Joey readily agreed to do this. He stepped into his canoe, untied it, and paddled off.

Holly and Ricky mounted their bicycles and pedaled in the direction of the Johnson farm. It was located on a hillside a little more than a mile away. They arrived ahead of Joey and waited for him.

Then the three climbed a rail fence and crossed a low hill into a large pasture. In it several animals were grazing at the end of long chains.

"See the antelopes?" Joey asked.

"Oh, they're only goats!" Ricky said.

"What's the difference," Joey replied, laughing. "They both have four legs and horns."

Holly did not care. She liked animals, and approached one of the goats to pet him. But as she did, the animal circled around her, pulling its chain along the grass.

"Look out, Holly, or you'll get tangled up," Ricky warned. Holly jumped and the chain passed under her feet, but the goat quickly ran around her again. This time Holly was caught.

"Help, help!" she cried out.

The chain pulled tighter around the little girl's legs. She cried out again, and fell to the ground.

CHAPTER 4

Travel Trouble

HOLLY screamed again as the chain bound tighter around her ankles. Ricky tried bravely to steer the goat in the opposite direction, but the animal was nearly as large as he was.

"Help us, Joey!" Ricky cried out. The big boy made no attempt to do so. Instead he stood laughing.

Holly's cries, however, reached Mr. Johnson, the farmer, who was setting out tomato plants in a nearby field. He came running.

"What's going on here?" the farmer demanded.

"My sister's caught!" Ricky exclaimed.

"Hold still, Billy," the farmer spoke to the goat and unsnapped the chain from its collar. When he released Holly's ankles, Joey started to run toward the fence. Now freed, Billy the goat ambled down the hill until he saw Joey running. Then Billy lowered his head and started pell-mell after the boy.

"Run, Joey, run!" Ricky cried.

Joey glanced over his shoulder. A look of fright came to his face, and he mustered all his speed. But the goat was faster.

Just as Joey reached the fence, Billy butted him with his horns. Joey sailed through the air, landing on the other side of the fence with a thud.

"Yikes, that must have hurt," Ricky said, wincing. He watched Joey pick himself up and limp off.

"Now tell me," Mr. Johnson said, helping Holly to her feet, "what are you doing here in my pasture?"

Ricky related Joey's story of the antelopes and added, "We shouldn't have believed him. He fooled us."

"Well, now," the farmer said, "you just follow me and we'll bathe this little girl's ankles in cold water."

They walked down the hillside, past the barn, and into the kitchen of the rambling old farmhouse. Mr. Johnson called his wife, and she filled a tub with cold water. Holly removed her shoes and socks and bathed her feet.

"Thank you. You're very sweet," she said.

"How would you like some cold goat's milk and cookies?" Mrs. Johnson asked kindly.

Holly and Ricky nodded vigorously. The farm woman gave them tall glasses of rich, creamy milk and a plateful of oatmeal cookies.

"I'm sorry we jumped over your fence and bothered the goats," Holly said after her tongue wiped away a little milk mustache.

"Me too," Ricky apologized. "Yikes, this is good!"

Mrs. Johnson dried Holly's feet and soon the two children were ready to leave. The farmer accompanied them to the gate, said good-by, and then hurried off to catch Billy and chain him in the pasture again.

Later, at supper, when Pete and Pam heard of the adventure with the goats, they felt sorry for their sister, and for Joey too.

"Don't be disappointed about the antelopes," Pam said. "We'll see some out West."

"When are we going?" Ricky asked.

"Tomorrow morning," Mrs. Hollister answered. "You'd all better scoot off to bed early."

Everybody was up at six o'clock the next morning. They put last-minute things in the suitcases, and Pete and Ricky sat on them to get them closed. Domingo, Zip, White Nose, and her kittens were to remain at the house, where Mr. Hollister would feed them daily.

By eight o'clock the station wagon was packed and ready to go. The girls hugged and kissed their father and promised to write post cards along the way.

As the car pulled out of the driveway, Pam spied Joey Brill walking stiffly down the street.

"Good-by, Joey!" they called out, as the station wagon passed him.

"Ha ha!" Joey called back. "You're going to have trouble on this trip."

"What does he mean by that?" Pete asked, as his mother continued on toward the main highway.

Mrs. Hollister thought it was just an unkind remark which meant nothing.

Joey's prediction about trouble did not come true— at least not for the first two days of the cross-country drive. Happy hours were spent in a leisurely tour as the family crossed the eastern mountains and glided over the long ribbons of highway stretching through the central states. For the first two nights Mrs. Hollister selected motels that had swimming pools, and the children took a refreshing dip in the early evening.

The third day out, however, was not so tranquil. In the middle of the afternoon the weather became cloudy. Then rain swept down, and even the rapidly swishing windshield wipers were unable to cope with the torrent.

Mrs. Hollister pulled to the side of the road and waited the storm out.

The car following behind her did the same.

After the rain had let up, Mrs. Hollister started on her way and the car behind did likewise.

"Let's stop at a motel earlier today," Pam said. "You must be very tired."

"I guess you're right, Pam," Mrs. Hollister replied. It was four o'clock by now, and patches of blue could be seen through the clearing skies.

Mrs. Hollister pulled up in front of a modern motel and parked. It was built on the side of the road, and the land behind it sloped down gradually into a large field studded with boxes.

After the family carried the luggage into their adjoining rooms, Holly looked out the back window.

"Mother, what are those boxes?" she asked.

"Those are beehives," came the reply. "The motel people raise honey and sell it to tourists."

Ricky and Pete entered the room occupied by their mother and sisters. "Yikes," said Ricky, "this is a keen place to stay."

"It's lovely," Pam agreed. She stood by the open window, beside which was a writing desk. On it were some post cards.

"I think I'll write Daddy a note," Mrs. Hollister said. She opened her purse to get her pen, and at the same time removed her new wallet in which she kept stamps.

"Tell Daddy how much we miss him," Holly said as her mother began to write.

Mrs. Hollister opened her wallet, removed a stamp, and set the beautifully initialed billfold on the window sill. Then, as she unclasped her purse to replace it, suddenly a man's hand reached in the window.

Pam screamed with fright. Mrs. Hollister was so stunned she could not move.

But Pete did. He sprang across the room and grasped the hand just as the fingers closed around the wallet.

"Stop thief!" Pete cried out. But with a powerful wrench, the man jerked free of Pete's grasp and the boy fell back. Then a scuffle of running feet could be heard outside. By the time Pete got to his feet and looked out the window no one was in sight.

"Oh dear!" cried Mrs. Hollister, her face pale.

"Don't worry, Mother!" Pete reassured her. "We'll find the thief." He dashed out of the room, followed by Pam, Holly, and Ricky. Pete hastened directly to the motel office and reported what had happened. The motel manager, an elderly man with gray hair and gold-rimmed glasses, helped the children search about the motel, but they could find no one. Now Mrs. Hollister and Sue, too, joined in looking, but it was no use. As

"Stop thief!"

the manager escorted them back to their rooms, he apologized to the children's mother for the unpleasant incident.

"I'll telephone the police," he promised.

"We'll go with you," Pete volunteered. "Maybe we'll find a clue in the office." Pete, Pam, Holly, and Ricky followed the manager. While he called headquarters, they looked around the room quietly.

Just as the manager put down the telephone, there was a loud crash in front of the motel. Pete dashed out to see what it was. "Crickets!" he cried out. "A car has crashed into our station wagon!"

"Goodness!" gasped the manager as he hurried out. "What next!"

The rear of the Hollister station wagon was dented by the front of another car which had rammed into it.

Mrs. Hollister rushed out to see what had happened. A short, bald, wiry man stepped out of the car, waving his arms wildly.

"You backed into me!" he cried out.

"Oh, what a fib!" shouted Holly. "Mother did nothing of the sort!"

Mrs. Hollister was flabbergasted by the false accusation. "Of course I did not back into you," she said. "I was in my room."

At that moment the policeman whom the manager had summoned arrived on the scene in a squad car. As he stepped out, the short bald-headed man strode over to him and said, "I demand that this woman be arrested. She damaged my car."

The policeman walked over to Mrs. Hollister and said, "Madam, may I see your license and car registration?"

"I don't have them," said Mrs. Hollister. "My wallet was just stolen."

The bald-headed man made a scoffing sound. "That's a good story! I don't think she even has a license."

"What's your name?" Pete asked the stranger.

"Murch—Otis Murch," he said, reaching into his pocket. He pulled out a wallet and displayed his license.

The policeman examined it. "I see you're from Colorado," the policeman said.

Pete hurried around to the back of the car. Sure enough, the license plate said Colorado.

Pam hurried back to him. "This looks like the same car that passed us so slowly when the Blairs had the blowout," she said excitedly.

"And it could be the same one Indy saw the prowler get away in," Pete replied.

"But we're not absolutely sure," Pam added, "so we'd better not say anything to the policeman." Meanwhile the officer was talking with Mrs. Hollister. "I'm afraid you'll have to come to headquarters," he said, "and tell us more details about the theft."

"I doubt there was any theft," Mr. Murch said. "She should be fined for not having her license."

"Oh, you're a fibber!" Ricky declared.

Mrs. Hollister smiled and said, "I'll go to headquarters, Officer, if Mr. Murch will."

"Sure I'll go!" the unpleasant man snapped. "I'll tell how you backed into my car."

Sue and Holly were in tears by now, and Pam put her arms about them.

"We'll stay here until you return, Mother," Pete said. "I'll take care of things."

Mr. Murch backed his car up and parked it alongside the Hollisters'. Then he and the children's mother entered the police car and drove off.

"Please don't cry," Pam told the youngsters. "Why don't you go and play?"

"I have an idea," Pete said. "How about inspecting the beehives?"

"Okay," Ricky agreed. "Come on, kids."

The three youngsters hurried off down the hill behind the motel, while Pete and Pam stood looking at Mr. Murch's car.

"That man certainly is mean," Pam said.

"He's up to something," Pete agreed. "And I'm going to find out what." He looked into the front window of the car, but could see nothing suspicious. Then he looked into the back seat. Something bright and shiny lay on the floor.

"Pam, come look at this," Pete called. He opened the door, reached in, and pulled out a shiny object.

When Pam saw it she gasped. "Pete!" she cried. "It's a broken initial from Mother's wallet!"

CHAPTER 5

A Suspicious Stranger

"Murch is the thief!" Pete exclaimed as he examined the broken initial.

"We have to catch him!" said Pam, her eyes flashing. The two children discussed how they might do this.

"I don't think we should leave here," Pete reasoned. "If we got someone to give us a ride to the police station, Murch might pass us coming back."

They agreed that they would wait until Murch, their mother, and the patrolman returned. "Then we can have him nabbed before he gets into his car," Pete declared.

They pulled two chairs in front of their motel rooms and waited.

"Why is Murch doing this to us?" Pam wondered.

"Perhaps he's an enemy of the Blairs," Pete said, "and is trying to keep us from helping them solve the mysteries."

While Pete and Pam kept their gaze fixed on the motel driveway, Holly, Ricky, and Sue went skipping into the pasture behind the motel. When they ran through a patch of daisies, Holly and Sue stopped to pick some for their mother. Then they continued on to the beehives. Sue walked close to watch several of the insects buzzing around the box before flying into it.

"See the cute little doorway!" Sue exclaimed. Just as she pointed, a bee lighted on her finger. Sue screamed as it stung her.

Her cries were so loud that Pete and Pam, sitting in front of the motel, heard them.

"Sue's in trouble!" Pam cried. Pete bounded out of his chair, and his sister followed him. They raced down the grassy slope behind the motel and soon were at the side of little Sue. She held up her finger for them to see. It was red and swollen.

"We need some mud," said Pam. This was not the first time one of the Hollister children had been stung, and Pam knew exactly what to do.

"Look over there." Ricky indicated a little marshy glen surrounded by three graceful willow trees. The children hastened to the spot and found a tiny spring welling out of the ground. Pam bent down to scoop up a little mud. She daubed it on Sue's finger, then bound it loosely with her handkerchief.

"All better now?" Holly asked, smiling.

"The hurt is all gone," Sue remarked as she wiped away her tears with the back of her hand. "It only tickles a little bit now."

The five children trudged up the slope. When they turned the corner of the motel Pete cried out in dismay. Mrs. Hollister stood talking to the policeman. But Murch and his car had vanished.

"Mother!" Pam shouted, running up to them. "Where did Mr. Murch go?"

Mrs. Hollister smiled and said, "It has all been straightened out, dear. Mr. Murch admitted he made a mistake and apologized. He drove off a few minutes ago."

"But Mother, he's the thief!" Pete declared. "Look at this!" He thrust his hand in his pocket and drew out the telltale initial from Mrs. Hollister's stolen wallet.

"Where did you find that?" the policeman asked.

"In Murch's automobile."

Without another word, the patrolman went to his car and broadcast an alarm for Otis Murch. Then he returned and began searching the ground where the thief's car had been parked.

"Are you looking for the wallet?" Pete asked him.

"Yes," came the reply. "Thieves don't usually keep things like that. They get rid of them as quickly as possible."

When Ricky heard this, he hastened to a wastebasket in the motel office and rummaged through it. Moments later he ran back outside crying, "I've found it! Here's your purse, Mother!"

The policeman strode over to Ricky and examined the wallet. Part of the broken initial remained attached to it.

"There's no money here, Mrs. Hollister," the officer reported, "but everything else looks intact." Then he tilted back his cap and scratched his head. "Wonder what this fellow's motive was?" he said aloud.

"Robbery, of course," Mrs. Hollister replied.

"It was more than that!" Pete said hotly. "Why did he ram into our car and blame you, Mother?"

"He may be trying to keep you from making your trip for some reason," suggested the officer. "Who would want to stop you?"

50

"I can't think of anyone," Mrs. Hollister replied. "Besides, we made up our minds about it so quickly that only the family and a few friends knew we were leaving."

Ricky and Holly exchanged a look.

After the policeman had left, Ricky told the family Joey Brill's story that a stranger had questioned him about the Hollisters.

"Maybe there really was a man asking about us, and Joey told him about our trip," Holly said.

"And perhaps Murch is the man," Ricky added.

"I'll bet that's what Joey meant when he yelled that we were going to have trouble," Pete remarked.

Mrs. Hollister looked thoughtful. A little later she wrote a long letter to her husband, telling of the incident. Then the family had supper in the motel restaurant. They had finished and were returning to their rooms when the policeman came back.

"We found Murch's car abandoned on a highway forty miles from here," he said. "It wasn't really his. The auto was rented in Colorado."

"I hope you can catch that old meanie," Holly declared.

"We'll keep trying," the officer promised, adding, "We've already sent out an alarm to several states."

Next morning Mrs. Hollister cashed a check to replenish her supply of money and they set off again. After several hours of driving through the cool, fresh prairie, they began to climb higher and higher to the foothills of the Rocky Mountains.

All during the day Mrs. Hollister kept glancing into her rear-view mirror, and Pete constantly checked the road behind them. But no suspicious cars appeared, and they saw nothing of Mr. Murch.

Tired, but excited about approaching Nevada, the Hollisters stayed at a small motel high in a mountain pass. At daybreak they were on their way again.

"If we're lucky, we'll reach Elkton by evening," Mrs. Hollister said.

Driving along in bright sunlight, Ricky suddenly exclaimed, "Yikes! Where did all the trees go?" The change in scenery had been so gradual that nobody recalled exactly when they had left the trees and green fields behind them.

On all sides now stretched a vast open land, rimmed with distant white mountain peaks. Low juniper bushes, sagebrush, and tumbleweed stretched away as far as they could see. The road before them became a thin white ribbon, rising and falling in tiny waves until it disappeared on the horizon.

"We're in the great wild West now," Pete announced. They drove on for several hours until Mrs. Hollister approached a fork in the road. The sun glinted off the signpost, and she slowed down to look at it.

"Elkton to the right," said Pam.

"No, to the left," Ricky urged.

Their mother turned left, as this had been the last direction given her.

"Are you sure now, Ricky?" she asked.

"Why don't we go back and look?" Pam suggested.

"I may have been wrong, Mother," Ricky admitted.

"Let's not lose any time," Pete said. "We'll know soon enough if we're on the wrong road."

"Look, an animal's chasing us!"

Mrs. Hollister drove five or six miles. The road was good, but no cars met them from the opposite direction. As frown lines appeared on Pam's forehead, Sue suddenly cried out, "Look, an animal's chasing us!"

All eyes turned to see a graceful four-legged creature running along the side of the road, keeping up with their car.

"It must be an antelope!" Pete exclaimed. He could see the cinnamon-buff body of the beautiful animal, its white underside and sharply contrasting black and white face. The children could barely make out the two tiny horns on either side of its head near the long pointed ears.

"Come on, Mom, race him!" Ricky called out.

By now the road had narrowed, and Mrs. Hollister was driving about forty miles an hour. The antelope kept pace for a while, and then veered off to join two others loping gracefully in the sagebrush several hundred yards from the road.

"Aren't they beautiful!" cried Pam.

"But I don't see any babies," Sue piped up.

Now their mother stopped the car. Turning it around, she said, "Pam, I think you were right," and added, "Ricky, you should learn to read signs better."

"But I knew we were going to see an antelope," Ricky remarked impishly. He rested his chin on the back of the front seat. Pete, who was riding next to his mother, turned and mussed up his brother's red hair.

"Well, anyhow," Pam said as they reached the fork in the road again, "we had lots of fun getting lost."

After a quick lunch at a small roadside restaurant, the Hollisters climbed into their station wagon and continued their journey. Their eyes grew weary scanning the sagebrush for more antelope, but they saw none in the flat desert area they were crossing.

At three o'clock, the travelers entered a small town which a signpost announced as Salt Creek. The main street had small shops on either side, and a few cars were parked diagonally at the curb. When Mrs. Hollister halted at a stop light, Ricky glanced across the street at a building a few doors ahead with a sign reading: SHERIFF'S OFFICE.

"Oh, look at that!" he said, pointing. "Just like on TV."

As he spoke, the light turned green and the station wagon moved on. But also at that moment the sheriff's door opened. A roughly dressed man ran out, vaulted into the front seat of an old jalopy, made a U turn, and sped off down the highway in front of the Hollisters.

"Mother!" Holly cried. "That's a fugitive, and he's getting away!"

CHAPTER 6

The Mysterious Cowboy

"Follow that car!" Ricky ordered. "Don't let the bandit get away!"

Holly's imagination was equal to Ricky's. "He really looked like a bad man, Mommy!" she cried. In her mind's eye, Holly saw the sheriff of Salt Creek sprawled on the floor behind his desk with a smoking pistol in his hand.

"My goodness, children," Mrs. Hollister said, driving along at a reasonable rate of speed. "That man is probably just a friend of the sheriff's."

Pam agreed. "Just because he's in a hurry doesn't mean he's a bad man, Holly."

"Well, I think he is," Sue chirped, " 'cause Ricky thinks so."

"That makes it a tie vote, three to three," Pete said with a chuckle, "so we just won't do anything about chasing the desperado."

Yet there were other things to interest the travelers. From time to time a huge jack rabbit would bound across the road. Several times the children saw tiny prairie dogs. They looked like miniature ground hogs sitting alertly beside the little holes they had dug in the desert.

For a few miles the road paralleled a railroad track. A train caught up with the Hollisters' car. As it passed by, the children merrily waved at the passengers, who smilingly returned their greeting.

Finally, on a distant flat, they saw Elkton, with its skyscraper, five stories high, standing out like a sentinel against the blue-gray mountains behind it. With mounting excitement, the children watched the toy-sized buildings grow larger as they drew closer to the town.

At last Mrs. Hollister drove over the railroad tracks and entered the main street. "Now we have to find directions to the Tumbling K," she said. As she drove along slowly, the children looked for signs pointing to the Blairs' ranch but could see none.

Suddenly Ricky cried out, "I see him! There he goes!"

"Who?" Pete asked.

"The bad guy! The man who got away at Salt Creek!" Ricky said, pointing to an alley between two stores.

Their mother intended to stop, but not to search for the stranger. Instead she pulled into a service station. Instantly Ricky and Holly jumped out. They ran down the street and into the alley, but returned in a moment, out of breath.

"He disappeared," panted Ricky.

"Lucky for him," Pam said with a wink at Pete. "You and Holly would have arrested him for sure."

The younger Hollisters took the teasing with a smile. Then, while their mother had the attendant check the gas and oil, Sue declared, "I'm hot—and thirsty."

"There's a soda shop across the street," Mrs. Hollister said. "Why don't you get yourselves a treat?"

Pete took the money his mother offered, then crossed the street with his brother and sisters. The soda shop felt cool and smelled sweet. The five youngsters walked to the counter, slid onto the stools, and spun around while waiting for the clerk to serve them.

Just then another girl, about Pam's age, entered and sat beside her. She wore a frilly cotton dress, and every curl in her brown hair was neatly in place.

"Hello," Pam said in a friendly tone. The girl looked Pam up and down, from her fluffy windswept hair to her dungarees and sneakers. She did not reply, but turned her head away quickly, nose in the air.

"Such friendly people out here," said Holly, sitting on the other side of Pam.

The clerk, who had been clearing dishes in a nearby booth, stepped behind the counter and grinned at the Hollisters. "All brothers and sisters, I can see that," he said.

"Don't include me," the brown-haired girl said. "I don't belong with those saddle tramps." Her mouth turned down at the corners, and she frowned crossly.

Sue looked at her sadly and said, "You're smiling upside down."

The others burst out laughing, whereupon the girl quickly moved one stool away from Pam.

"She's stuck up," Holly whispered, and in a louder voice said, "I'd like a chocolate sundae with vanilla ice cream and nuts and chocolate syrup and whipped cream on top."

Pam gave a startled cry.

"Make it two," Ricky chimed in. Sue ordered strawberry ice cream, while Pam and Pete asked for vanilla milk shakes. The girl in the dress wanted a soda.

The clerk served the Hollisters first.

"Umm, isn't this good!" Ricky declared.

Just then Pam let out a startled cry, which was followed by a crash of glass. Her neighbor's soda had slipped from the counter, spilled over Pam's jeans, and crashed on the tile floor.

"See what you made me do!" the girl cried angrily.

Pam was thunderstruck. "What do you mean?" she asked, wiping a blob of ice cream from her jeans with a napkin.

"You made me so nervous my hand slipped," the girl said. Then, without a word of apology, she slid off the stool and hurried out of the store.

"Hey, wait!" the clerk called. He shook his head. "She's a spoiled kid."

The clerk got a mop, dustpan, and broom. With them he swept up the broken glass and cleaned the floor.

"I'm sorry about what happened," he said. "That girl lives in a hotel in town. She's a queer one."

Pam wiped the spilled drink from her jeans, but it left a large damp spot.

"I'd like to make it up to you somehow," the clerk said. With that he dipped down into the ice cream containers and gave each of the children an extra scoop.

"Well, crickets! Thanks!" Pete said.

When they had finished, Pete paid the bill and the children hurried to the gas station, where their mother was waiting for them.

When Pam told her what had happened, Mrs. Hollister said, "There are some rude people in this world, but fortunately not too many." She added, "The attendant here gave me directions to the Tumbling K. It's not far. Hop in."

The road they took ran south of town several miles. Then it turned right and headed directly into the rolling foothills. It twisted and turned, finally leading them into a plateau-like clearing.

"Look, there's the ranch!" Pete called out. Before them was a long, low house made of logs. It was shaded by a clump of cottonwood trees. Off to one side was a horse barn, and next to it a large corral.

As the car drew closer, the children could see a tall water tank looming up among the trees behind the barn. And, much to their surprise, they spied a little pond in a green field to the right of the ranch house. It was fed by a lively stream. A small dam cascaded a silvery sheet of water into a meadow, where cattle were grazing.

As they drove through a large gate they saw a post beside it. On it was burned a leaning letter K.

Pete, who was riding in front, reached over and honked the horn several times.

Instantly, out of the barn ran two children.

"Look! Bunky and Gina!" Holly cried.

"And there's Mr. Blair coming out of the house!"

When Mrs. Hollister stopped the car in front of the ranch house, the youngsters flung open the doors and jumped out like exploding firecrackers.

"Here we are!" Ricky announced.

The boys slapped one another on the back, and the girls exchanged hugs. As they did, a short, slender, dark-haired woman came from the house. Mr. Blair introduced his wife to the Hollisters.

"You have a lovely place here," Mrs. Hollister remarked, looking about and breathing deeply of the thin crisp air.

"Only one trouble," Mr. Blair replied. "Not enough rain for profitable grazing."

"But you haven't met the whole outfit," Mrs. Blair said, smiling. "Here come some of the others."

A husky, handsome man with a slightly bowlegged walk, and a pretty bright-eyed girl with titian hair, came slowly from the corral.

"Meet Bronc Callahan, our foreman," Mr. Blair said. "This is his daughter, Cindy."

They shook hands, and the youngsters chatted with the girl, who Pam guessed to be about sixteen.

"Cindy works part time at the Elkton library," Gina said. "She brings us good books."

"You had me fooled for a moment," Mr. Blair said. "When I saw your car, I thought it was the new cowboy I'm going to hire."

For the next half hour Gina, Bunky, and Cindy showed the Hollisters around the ranch headquarters, while the grownups stayed at the house, talking. The children marveled at the pond, which they were told was full of fish. While they were looking down into a deep barbecue pit, Pete suddenly asked, "Say, where's Old Dad Callahan?"

"Oh, he's lion hunting," Bunky answered. He told them that a mountain lion had been killing calves.

As they all walked back to the house, a second car arrived. When its driver stepped out, Holly gave a little gasp. "Ricky," she asked, "isn't that the bad man who got away?"

"Yikes! It looks like him," Ricky said. He whispered their suspicions to Pete, Pam, and Mrs. Hollister. But their mother did not interrupt the meeting between the new arrival and Mr. Blair.

"I'm Dakota Dawson," the tall cowboy drawled.

"Welcome," Mr. Blair replied, shaking his hand.

Dakota Dawson looked down at the children, who were studying him intently. He had a lean jaw, weather-beaten face, and gray eyes. When Mr. Blair introduced him to the Hollisters, Dakota merely nodded his head. Then he opened the trunk of his car and pulled out his saddle and bedroll.

Ricky stepped over to him and said, "Dakota, do you come from Salt Creek?"

The mysterious cowboy looked at his questioner without smiling. Then he replied, "I have a brother who lives there." With one hand he carried the bedroll, with the other he swung the saddle over his shoulder and strode into the bunkhouse.

Perplexed by the strange cowboy's abrupt manner, Holly and Ricky tagged along behind the others as they were ushered into the ranch house. They passed into the shade of a long portico, then entered a big living room. The beamed ceiling, Pam could see, was of hand-hewn timbers. At one end stood a huge fireplace. At the other end, a corner used as a dining area contained a large round table.

Mrs. Hollister and Sue were directed to the guest room. Holly and Pam found twin cots set up in Gina's bedroom, and Pete and Ricky took their things to Bunky's quarters.

Then they all sat down to a tasty ranch dinner. By the time they had finished, darkness had fallen. The children strolled about the ranch, looking up at the brightly shining stars.

Pete's gaze fell to the huge dark shape of the mountains in the distance. He stopped and stared hard. He had seen a light! It flickered on and off. Never taking his eyes from it, Pete began walking slowly in the direction of the mountain.

Suddenly two powerful hands seized him by the shoulders!

CHAPTER 7

A Pig-tailed Fish

STRONG sinewy hands held Pete in a vise-like grip. As the boy struggled, a tall man pulled him back several yards.

"Let me go!" Pete cried out. He squirmed and struggled and tried to get a look at his captor. But the broad brim of the man's cowboy hat concealed his face in shadow. Now, in the bright moonlight, Pete thought he recognized the figure of Dakota Dawson.

"I know it's you, Dakota!" Pete said, and the powerful hands released him.

"Take it easy," came the reply. The cowboy tilted his hat, and the dim light showed the strong chin and weather-beaten features of the mysterious cowboy.

"What are you going to do to me?" Pete asked.

"Nothing." He pointed a few yards ahead to what appeared to be a black shadow beneath a towering cottonwood tree. "That's a barbecue pit. You were about to step into it."

"You saved me from getting hurt!" Pete said.

"Sure 'nuff. Never tramp around at night with your head in the air."

"But I was looking at the li—" Pete bit off the word. The lights, he thought, could be a signal to Dakota

Dawson or to some other persons operating illegally in the area of the Tumbling K Ranch.

Pete glanced toward the mountaintop again. The lights had flickered out. He turned to speak to Dakota, but now there was no one standing beside him. The cowboy had melted away into the shadows as mysteriously as he had appeared.

Walking back to the ranch house, Pete was puzzled over Dakota's behavior. Was he a spy for the mysterious mountain prowlers? Even if he was, Pete felt certain the man had some good qualities. "Otherwise," he thought, "he'd have let me fall into the barbecue pit and maybe get hurt."

Pete found Pam, Bunky, and Gina chatting near the porch. After he had told them what had happened, Bunky said, "When Old Dad comes back from his lion hunt, I'm going to tell him about Dakota. He has a way of figuring people out."

"But he hasn't been able to figure out Millie Simpson," Gina reminded him.

"That's right," her brother agreed. "If Millie saw those lights from her hotel window in town, she'll be too scared to take her riding lesson tomorrow."

"Where does she ride?" Pam asked.

"Out here on the ranch," Bunky replied. "Cindy, or Bronc, or sometimes Old Dad teaches her, but she doesn't pay any attention to us."

"Just the same I'd like to meet her," Pam said.

"Why?" Bunky asked.

"Just curious," Pam answered with a pleasant smile.

The four children had a snack of hot chocolate and cookies before they went to bed.

The next morning was bright and sparkling, as were most of the days in Nevada. The children rose early, had a hearty breakfast, and hurried to the corral to see the horses. Sue climbed to the top of the fence like the rest of them.

Inside the corral were a dozen pretty horses. Bronc Callahan, riding a spirited palomino, was swinging his lasso. He roped two gentle mounts and led them to the place where Pete and Pam were sitting.

"Pam," he said, "which one would you like to ride?"

"The little pinto," she replied.

"How about you, Pete? This buckskin horse all right?"

Pete nodded happily. "Yessir!"

"Well then," Bronc ordered, "hop down and lead them out of the corral. Then we'll saddle up for your first lesson in riding and roping."

"Crickets!" Pete exclaimed. "That's great!"

"Oh, thank you, Mr. Callahan!" said Pam, hopping down and leading her horse by the halter.

"Just call me Bronc." The foreman grinned down at them.

Even though Pete and Pam both were good riders, they were thrilled to have a lesson on the ranch. Bunky hastened to open the corral gate; and when Pete and Pam had led their horses to the bunkhouse, he and Gina carried out blankets and saddles.

"Will you teach us how to make a Mother Hubbard loop?" Pete asked.

"That depends on how fast you learn to make a smaller loop," replied Bronc, as the three rode toward the grassy meadow. Near the center of the meadow, a clump of cottonwoods grew next to the trickling stream. One old tree had been cut down, leaving a waist-high stump.

"That's our target," Bronc said. "Now take your ropes from the side of your saddle and build a loop like this."

Pete and Pam did as they were instructed. Then they rode back and forth, swinging their lariats toward the old stump. At first they missed, but after a while Pete's rope caught the stump.

"Yippee-aye-ee!" Pam cried out. "Pete, you're a real cowboy now."

Several turns later she caught the stump too. But Pam held on to the rope too tightly and was nearly pulled from her saddle.

In twisting around, however, Pam caught sight of another rider at the far end of the pasture. He was near the fringe of woods which stretched up the mountain slope.

The rider stopped and gazed at them a moment.

"Look, Pete!" Pam said. "There's Dakota Dawson!"

"Where's he going?" Pete asked the foreman.

"Out to mend fences."

"Do you know much about him?" Pete asked.

"He's a good cowboy. That's all." Then Bronc said, "Here's how you make a Mother Hubbard loop. Just let out a little more rope and swing it higher over your head."

While Pete and Pam were practicing, Ricky, Holly, and Sue wandered over to the ranch pond with Gina and Bunky.

"Yikes! This is keen!" Ricky said to Bunky, who was walking by his side. "Do you ever swim here?"

"No," the ranch boy replied. "The water's too cold."

"Then I know what we could do," Holly decided. "We could build a raft and have some fun."

"But I want to catch a fish," Sue objected.

"All right, honey," said Gina. "I'll get you a pole and some bait."

She hurried off to the house and returned a few minutes later with a fishing rod and a small plate containing a piece of cheese.

"Is the cheese for me?" Sue asked, looking surprised.

"It's for the fish," Gina replied.

"Yikes! Do you serve it to them on a plate?" Ricky asked.

"Of course not," said Bunky, grinning. He broke off a little piece of cheese and ran the fish hook through it.

"I didn't know fish liked cheese," Holly said.

"They love it, especially here out West," Gina declared.

Holly took hold of the rod and threw the line into the water. Then she put the pole in Sue's hands and turned to Bunky and Gina. "Do you have some wood we could make a raft with?"

"Sure. Right over there." Bunky pointed to logs neatly piled on the side of the ranch house next to the chimney. "We burn those in the fireplace," he said, "but I suppose you could use them to make a raft."

Leaving Sue to fish, the four others carried half a dozen logs to the side of the pond. Bunky ran to the barn and returned with an old clothesline. With it they lashed the logs together, then pushed the raft into the pond.

"Stop splashing!" Sue complained. "You'll scare the fish so they won't eat the cheese."

"All right," Holly said. "We'll be quiet."

Ricky was first to test the raft. He stepped on it gingerly. It bore his weight well. The red-haired boy dropped to his knees and, using his hands as paddles, propelled the raft into the middle of the pond. Then he leaned over to peer down into the water. The raft tilted, but Ricky quickly righted it again.

"I want a turn!" Holly called.

"Okay, here I come." Ricky paddled to shore and Holly stepped on the raft. Just as she reached the center of the pond, Sue cried out.

"I've got something!" The line had been tugged taut, and the tip of the rod bent and jerked.

"What a monster!" Gina exclaimed. "Reel it in, Sue!" But the little girl was too excited to do this. Instead, she let her line pay out more and more as the fish swam toward the opposite side of the pond.

"I'll help you, Sue," Holly volunteered. She leaned over the side to reach for the fish line. But as she did, the raft tilted. Holly tried to regain her balance. She teetered first one way, then the other, and with a shriek slipped off. Holly's feet hit the water first, but her head knocked against one of the logs.

"Yikes!" Ricky exclaimed, and Bunky and Gina cried out in alarm, as Holly slid beneath the surface of the cold water. A second later, her head and shoulders bobbed up, but Holly made no move to swim.

Holly teetered first one way, then the other.

"She's hurt!" wailed Sue, still hanging on to the fish pole.

Just then there came the sound of running feet behind her, and a moment later the large loop of a lariat fell into the water, neatly around Holly. It was quickly pulled tight about the girls' shoulders, and she was drawn to the side of the pond.

Ricky was surprised to see the man at the other end of the rope. He was an old fellow, whose white hair just showed beneath his cowboy hat. His face was broad and sunburned, and his blue eyes twinkled. As he knelt down to pull Holly out of the water, he said with a chuckle, "This is the first time I ever caught a fish with pigtails!"

Holly shivered. "Thanks for saving me," she said. "When I bumped my head I saw a million stars."

Nobody had been paying much attention to Sue, who was still struggling with her fish. The cowboy walked over with a rolling motion, and reeled in the catch. It was a large, wriggling, squirming trout.

"Another prize!" the man exclaimed. "But look, this one doesn't have pigtails!"

All the children laughed.

"Old Dad, you always make jokes!" Gina said, hugging the cowboy. Then she introduced the Hollisters.

"We've heard a lot about you," Holly told him, her teeth still chattering from the icy water.

"Well, git along into some dry clothes, and I'll tell you what happened to me!" Old Dad Callahan promised.

Holly hurried to the ranch house with Gina. While they were gone, Old Dad cleaned the fish, and Sue carried it proudly to the kitchen. "Well, good for you, Sue!" Mrs. Blair praised her. "I'll fry this for lunch, especially for you."

As the little girl skipped back to the others, she was followed by her sister and Gina. Holly was wearing a pair of the ranch girl's dungarees and a bright plaid shirt. Her pigtails were still damp, but she did not mind that.

Just behind the girls came Mrs. Hollister with her daughter's wet clothes, which she planned to hang in the sun. Gina introduced the children's mother to Old Dad, and Mrs. Hollister said, "I hope you'll excuse my wild Indians if they've been any trouble to you."

Old Dad tilted his sombrero back and scratched his head. "Ma'am," he said, "out here in the West we say, the wilder the colt, the better the hoss. Mighty fine children." He put an arm around Holly and Ricky. "About that adventure of mine. Come over here and I'll tell you all about it."

Old Dad led the children to a picnic table near the barbecue pit and sat down on a bench. "Now the mountain lion," he began, "gave me a hard time. The critter ran up a tree backward, and I didn't know which way to shoot."

"Old Dad!" Bunky said. "You're telling us another one of your tall stories."

"Well, maybe it didn't happen exactly that way," Old Dad admitted. "Anyhow, I didn't get the lion this time, but I will."

Then he paused and looked thoughtfully toward the mountaintop. "There's something awful mysterious going on up there," he remarked finally.

"That's why we're here!" Ricky piped up. "We're going to help you solve the mystery."

Old Dad shook his head slowly from side to side and stared at his boots. "That'll be dangerous for children," he said. "The woods are thick and gloomy, and who knows what might be hiding up there?"

"We don't get frightened," Holly declared.

"Oh, really?" Old Dad said, putting a hand in his pocket. "Well, we'll just see, young lady."

He pulled out something concealed in his large gnarled hand and gave it to Holly. She reached out for it, then let out a little shriek.

"Oh, what is it?" she exclaimed, holding a tiny, spiny-looking creature in her palm.

"That's a horny toad," Bunky said. "Where did you find it, Old Dad?"

"Down in the desert a ways."

"May I keep it?" Holly asked.

"Sure." But he added with a wink, "You know a horned toad isn't really a toad at all. It's a lizard."

"Just so long as it's friendly," Ricky said seriously as Holly gave him the horny toad to pet.

"Oh, horny toads won't hurt you," Bunky assured him. He looked admiringly at Holly. "You weren't scared, were you?"

"Just startled, I guess," she replied and laughed.

"Oh-oh, look who's coming," Bunky said, glancing toward the corral. A car stopped, and a young girl stepped out.

"Here comes Millie for her riding lesson," Gina said.

"Is that Millie Simpson?" Holly exclaimed.

"Sure. Do you know her?" Bunky asked.

"She's the girl who spilled the soda on Pam!" Holly declared hotly.

CHAPTER 8

Antelope Hunt

"MILLIE Simpson's a creep!" Ricky said, and told of the incident at the soda shop in Elkton.

"That sounds like something she'd do all right," Bunky declared. "Look, her mother's driving away. She'll come back to pick up Millie when the lesson's over."

As he spoke, Pete and Pam rode up with the ranch foreman. "Old Dad," Bunky said, "I'd like you to meet the rest of the Hollisters—Pete and Pam."

"Howdy, partners," Old Dad said, touching the edge of his sombrero. "I hope my son's taking good care of you."

"He's been teaching us how to ride and rope," Pete replied.

"And they're good pupils, too," Bronc commented.

Old Dad grinned until his eyes crinkled. "Just remember, young 'uns," he cautioned, "tossin' your rope before building the loop don't catch the calf."

Pam was delighted by the quaint expression. "You mean, don't do anything before you're ready," she remarked.

"That's it," Old Dad said. "Like tryin' to catch those mysterious yahoos up yonder before you know the lay of the land."

Just then Millie approached, dressed in jodhpurs and carrying a riding crop. "Bronc," she said in a demanding voice, "I want Cindy to give me my lesson today."

"Well, howdy," the foreman said. "Millie, I'd like you to meet the Hollisters."

Millie looked each of the Eastern children up and down, then repeated, "I want Cindy to ride with me today."

"I'm afraid that's impossible," Bronc told her, ignoring Millie's snub. "Cindy is working at the library."

"Then I won't take my lesson."

"That's up to you," Bronc replied with a shrug.

Pam spoke up. "I'll ride with you, Millie."

"Humph!" Millie said, tilting her chin up. "Who said you could ride?"

"I say so," Bronc answered quietly. "Pam is more advanced than you are, Millie. She'll be able to give you a good lesson."

Millie turned on her heel and strode off. But seeing that her mother had already left, she paused, hesitated, and turned back to where the other children looked on in disgust.

"I'll think it over!" she announced haughtily.

Pam took a few steps over to her. "Let's be friends, Millie," she said.

"Sure!" Ricky chimed in. "We even have a gift for you."

Before Pam or Pete knew what was happening, the girl put out her hand and Ricky plopped the horny toad into it. Millie let out a shriek that Ricky thought would surely be heard in Elkton.

"Ow, it bit me!" Millie cried, dropping the toad to the ground.

"Oh, Ricky!" Pam protested, as her brother picked up the lizard. "Why did you do that?"

" 'Cause I like her," he answered with a twinkle in his eyes.

Millie's face turned scarlet. She held her breath for several seconds. Then she flung herself into the dust and began kicking wildly and screaming.

"Oh dear, she's dying!" Sue cried, as tears came to her eyes.

"Of course she's not," Gina calmly assured the little girl. "Millie is having another one of her tantrums."

Hearing the noise, the two mothers ran from the ranch house. While Mrs. Blair tried to soothe Millie, Mrs. Hollister hurried back to the kitchen and quickly returned with a wet towel.

"She's got hysterics. Too bad," Ricky said. "And just on account of a little old horny toad."

After Millie had exhausted herself, she rose sobbing, while Mrs. Hollister bathed her face with the cool cloth.

"I feel sorry for her," Pam whispered to Pete. "She has no brothers or sisters to play with—that's the trouble."

Overhearing her say this, Old Dad commented, "I think she should be paddled."

"It's almost time for lunch now," Mrs. Blair put in. "You'd all better come in and get ready."

Pam stepped forward and put her arm around Millie's shoulder. "Come on, Millie," she said. "After we eat, we'll ride together. It'll be fun."

Millie did not protest this time. Instead, when the meal was over, she walked with Pam to the corral. They waited there while Bronc went into the pasture where the horses had been taken. He brought one back and saddled it for Millie.

Pam remounted her pinto, and the girls walked the animals around the inside of the corral. Bronc sat on the fence, making sure that nothing happened during the riding lesson.

Bunky and Gina, meanwhile, went with their mother to do some chores. Mrs. Hollister watched Millie for a moment, sighed, and returned to the house.

Pete, Ricky, Holly, and Sue followed Old Dad, and they all sat down in the shade of a cottonwood tree.

"Old Dad," Pete said, "any more news about baby antelopes being stolen?"

The old cowboy hunkered down, a piece of dried grass between his teeth.

"Those varmints have been quiet for a few days," he answered. "But if they continue to raid the valley, there won't be any antelopes left."

"Why can't you catch them?" Pete asked.

"There just aren't enough policemen or game wardens out here," he replied. "And the antelope thieves are slippery scoundrels."

"Maybe they have a hide-out in the mountains," Holly suggested.

"Could be," Old Dad agreed. "But nobody has been able to trace them."

"Tell us more about antelopes," Ricky begged.

Old Dad said that the white men had never heard of the animals until Lewis and Clark returned in 1806 from their expedition to the Pacific coast.

"In those days," the cowboy went on, "there were about forty million antelope in the Western grasslands from Mexico to Canada."

Pete whistled. "Are there many left now?"

"There are some, but not nearly enough," Old Dad explained. "That's why we're trying to build up the herds around here." He went on to say that the antelopes, called "pronghorns" because of their two small horns, were the fastest four-legged creatures on the continent.

"Oh, I'd love to see an antelope baby," Holly said.

"Well, maybe you will," Old Dad replied. "Sooner than you might expect." He told them that two men from the Game Department were going to visit him that afternoon. "Perhaps they can spot an antelope for you," he said.

Just then the children heard shouting from the corral.

"Stop him! Stop him!" Millie screamed.

Old Dad and the youngsters raced toward the enclosure. Inside, Millie's horse was rearing and plunging, while the girl held on frantically.

Bronc Callahan leaped down from the fence and ran toward the unruly animal. At the same time Pam urged her pinto alongside Millie's horse and grabbed the bridle.

"Quiet, boy!" she commanded, and he stopped rearing.

Now the foreman reached them and helped the girl dismount. "What happened?" he asked.

"Stop him! Stop him!" Millie screamed.

"He wouldn't do what I told him so I hit him with my crop," Millie said.

"That's no way to treat an animal!" Bronc scolded her, and she burst into tears.

Pam dismounted also and led the weeping Millie into the ranch house. There the girl dried her eyes. In a few minutes her mother arrived, and Pam and Mrs. Blair watched from the portico as they drove off together.

"Millie's all right," Pam said sympathetically. "She needs someone to be her friend."

Just then a pickup truck drove into the ranch and stopped in front of the house. Old Dad strode over with his rolling gait to meet it, and Pete, Ricky, Holly, and Sue tagged after him. Bunky and Gina soon came running.

Two men stepped out of the car. "Hi, Jack! Howdy, Smitty!" Old Dad called out to them.

The one named Jack was tall and wiry. Smitty was short and lean. Both wore binoculars slung over their shoulders. In the rear of the pickup truck the Hollisters saw two huge circular nets attached to ten-foot poles.

After introductions were made, Jack said, "We're on our way to tag some more pronghorned fawns. Thought you'd like to come along."

"May we go, too?" Holly asked.

Smitty laughed and said, "We'll take as many as we can pile in the pickup truck."

"Crickets!" Pete exclaimed, and hurried inside the house to ask his mother for permission.

"If Old Dad goes with you, you may join the men," she said. "But be careful of Sue."

"Thanks, Mother!" Pete said.

Gina and Bunky begged to go along, too.

"Okay, hop in, everybody," Smitty ordered as he slid behind the steering wheel. Old Dad sat between the two men, with Sue on his lap. The other children scrambled into the back.

The truck rumbled down the winding ranch road and finally reached the main highway, which stretched across the floor of the valley. Halfway to the other side, Smitty turned off into the brush.

They bounced along for a few hundred yards and stopped. Then Jack climbed on top of the cab. Putting his binoculars to his eyes, he gazed out over the flat land.

"Smitty," he called out finally, "I see a pair of fawns!" He quickly got back into the cab and directed the driver, who proceeded slowly across the rough ground. Shortly Smitty stopped the car. He and Jack got the two big nets from the back and tiptoed through the sagebrush.

The children stood up and looked on, awestruck.

"I can't see a thing," Ricky complained. The youngsters climbed over the side of the truck and dropped to the ground.

"That's because the animals lie low against the earth," Old Dad told them.

Now the children followed the two men, walking as quietly as possible. After a while Pam whispered, "Pete, look! I see one over there!"

When Jack and Smitty heard her, they walked stealthily toward the spot, lifted their nets cautiously and *plop!* down they came over two young antelopes.

The children crowded up to get a close look.

"How funny!" Ricky declared. "Their heads are so large!"

"And they have such big ears!" Sue chirped.

The wardens gently removed the nets from the trembling creatures, then attached red tags to their ears.

"Oh, don't hurt them!" Pam protested.

"They can hardly feel it," Smitty replied. He explained that the animals were tagged so that the movements of the antelope herds could be determined.

"It's all in our program of conservation," Jack added.

Sue and Holly bent down to pat the fawns.

"I judge they're three days old," said Jack.

Just then Pete, who had stood up to gaze across the valley, suddenly shouted, "Look! There's another truck over yonder!"

Smitty wheeled around and put the glasses to his eyes. "The antelope thieves!" he exclaimed. "They're stealing a fawn!"

CHAPTER 9

A Strange Mark

"THE antelope thieves!" Pete cried. "Come on, let's get them!"

Jack and Smitty released the fawns they had tagged, and everyone hurried back to the truck. Jack started the motor, while his partner threw the nets in the rear and the passengers piled in. Smitty swung into the front seat, and they sped across the prairie.

Sue sat upon Old Dad's knees and cried out, "Faster! Faster! We want to catch the bad men."

"Looks like they got themselves a pronghorn all right," the old cowboy remarked, peering through Smitty's binoculars.

"They've seen us, too," Jack said. "They're racing toward the highway."

"I think we'll get them this time," Smitty declared as the truck churned up a cloud of dust.

Seated in the rear, the six other children shouted encouragement to the driver as the gap between the two trucks became smaller and smaller.

"They're driving a jeep!" Pete shouted, leaning over the side with the wind rushing into his face. Just then he cried out in despair, "Oh! They dropped an antelope out of the jeep!"

"Those mean men!" Pam said with a gasp. "How could they be so cruel?"

As the thieves probably had guessed it would, the truck slowed to a stop. The baby antelope lay on its side, kicking and whimpering. The jeep meanwhile had turned into the main highway and roared off in the direction of the Ruby Mountains.

Quickly they all got out of the truck. Smitty bent over the fawn, gently feeling its forelegs and hind legs.

"Nothing broken," he announced finally. "But this little doe is pretty well banged up." Her tender coat had been badly scraped on the side which hit the dirt road.

"Oh, if we only had some water to bathe her," Pam said.

"You'll find a canteen on the front seat," Smitty told her.

Pam ran to get it. Then she tore off a piece of her shirt tail and, moistening it with the water, bathed the injured animal.

But even after Pam's gentle treatment, the doe was barely able to stand. She wobbled and seemed dazed.

"Well, Smitty," said Jack, shaking his head sadly, "what are we going to do with her?"

"We're going to nurse her until she gets better," Pam spoke up quickly.

"Yes," Sue piped. "We know how to take care of animals, 'cause we have a dog and cats and a donkey."

Smitty smiled. "Well, Jack," he said, "that's the best offer you'll get today, so you'd better take it."

"It's unusual," his partner replied. Then he turned to Old Dad and asked, "Will you take the responsibility for this little critter?"

"Why, shore," Old Dad said. "These young 'uns'll take good care of her."

The two men gently lifted the trembling fawn into the back of the truck. But before Pete jumped in with the others, he examined the dusty road.

"What are you looking for?" Bunky asked.

"Tracks made by that jeep," Pete replied. "Here are some marks, but the treads don't show."

Smitty, as well as Bunky, became curious and studied the marks left by the getaway vehicle.

"Those are mighty fat tires," Pete observed. "Why would they use them?"

"For traveling over rough places," Bunky surmised.

"Say, I have an idea," Pete said, snapping his fingers. "Maybe they use smooth tires so the police can't pick up their tread patterns."

"Come on, fellas," Old Dad said. "We have to get this fawn to the Tumbling K. She needs some salve and a warm place to bed down."

Pete hopped into the back of the truck, and the game wardens headed back to the Blairs' ranch.

When they arrived, Gina and Bunky quickly prepared a bed of straw in one corner of the barn, and the fawn was laid carefully upon it.

Ricky and Sue watched over the little animal while the other children hastened into the ranch house. Pam, Holly, and Gina returned in a few moments. Gina carried a baby bottle of warm milk, and Pam brought a tube of ointment. While she spread the soothing balm over the scratches, Gina put the rubber nipple in the fawn's mouth.

"Look, she's drinking the milk!" Holly cried out in delight. "Now she'll get better."

"We'll have to give her a name," Ricky said.

"That's right," agreed Pam.

Several names were suggested, including Bouncy and Baby Doll.

Pam looked dreamily at the little pronghorn, which had now ceased trembling and gazed up at her with large luminous eyes.

"How do you like Prairie Star?" Pam asked. With that, the fawn pushed the nipple from her mouth and made a tiny bleating noise.

"Oh, lookee, she says 'Yes'!" Sue declared.

"That's a nice name, Pam," Holly agreed.

"Then let's call her Prairie Star," Gina said.

While the girls and Ricky were taking care of the little antelope, Jack and Smitty looked into the barn and said good-by. Then they drove off in their truck.

Pete, meanwhile, had hurried straight into the ranch house and telephoned the police in Elkton. He asked if the speeding jeep had been seen by any of their patrolmen. When he received a negative answer, Pete went out and looked for Old Dad. He found him beside the barn, currycombing one of the horses.

"I think we ought to track those hombres," Pete said. "We shouldn't let them get away with this."

"I'm with you, young detective," Old Dad replied. "How big a posse do you want?"

"I think just a few of us might be better than a whole troop," Pete said.

"That's right," the old cowboy agreed. "And we'd better start first thing in the morning."

"Bunky has promised to help his father tomorrow," Pete said, "but Ricky can go instead."

Early the next day, as they had planned, the three riders set off at a leisurely pace down the green plateau and along the winding road which led to the highway.

After a half-hour ride, Old Dad and the two boys came to the place where the jeep had driven onto the main highway.

"We better separate here," Old Dad said. "Suppose you two boys ride one side of the road, and I'll take the other. We have to find the spot where these yahoos turned off the highway—if they did." Now and again a car whizzed by, and jack rabbits scampered among the sagebrush. But the boys kept their eyes glued to the side of the road.

Finally them came to a low outcropping of rock which reached the edge of the highway on the boys' side. Pete reined up his horse.

"What do you see?" Ricky asked.

"Nothing right now," Pete replied. He called over to Old Dad, "This might be a good place for the jeep to turn off, because it wouldn't leave any marks on the rocks."

"You've got a smart idea there, buckaroo," Old Dad agreed, and crossed over the road to join the brothers.

Cautiously guiding their horses, the three riders proceeded over the rough rocky strip. Finally the stony area sank beneath the sand and brush of the prairie floor, which extended to the foot of the Ruby Mountains, a mile distant. Pete dismounted and examined the ground carefully. Ricky and Old Dad did the same.

Suddenly Ricky cried out, "Look Pete, what's this?"

His brother hurried to his side. A faint, wide track showed in the powdered dirt.

"Old Dad!" Pete exclaimed, "I think we've found the trail!"

The cowboy examined the marks closely and said, "Buckin' broncs, if you aren't right! Those fellows drove real slow on their smooth tires, but they didn't fool you boys."

Mounted again, the trio followed the tracks, which now became more distinct as the fugitive jeep had picked up speed.

As they rode along three abreast, Old Dad grinned and said, "Nobody's been able to trace these critters before, but we've picked 'em up, thanks to you, Pete." Then he went on, "As cowboys say, brains in the head save blisters on the feet."

Now the ground sloped up and met a fringe of juniper trees. Beyond them the pine woods colored the hillside a deep green. From nearby came the gurgle of running water.

"What's that?" Pete asked, halting his mount.

"Icy River," Old Dad answered, pointing off to his right. "It runs through Rustler's Canyon."

"The tracks are turning that way, too," Pete said.

Soon they came to a bubbling mountain stream. At its widest point it was fifteen feet across.

"I think we've found the trail."

"You call this a river?" Ricky asked, scratching his head.

"Out West here, they do," Old Dad said with a chuckle. "I guess you'd call it a creek back home."

Icy River, Old Dad told them, originated high in the Ruby Mountains. Starting as a mere trickle from melting snow, it picked up several rivulets, finally growing into a full-sized Western river.

Following the tire tracks beside the gurgling stream, the three riders worked their way uphill until they came upon a clearing. Pete, who was in the lead, held up his hand for silence.

"Look over there!" he whispered to Old Dad.

In the distance a cowboy was standing next to a pine tree.

"It's Dakota Dawson!" Pete said.

"Did he see us?" Ricky asked.

"I don't think so."

Old Dad and the boys backed their horses into the cover of some foliage and watched the cowboy. Dakota was looking intently at something on the tree. Then he walked over to his horse, mounted, and disappeared into the woods.

"Come on!" Pete said excitedly. "Let's find out what he was looking at."

A few minutes later they reached the tree and Pete gasped at what he saw. A crude X sign had been cut into the bark.

"It's a message of some kind!" he guessed.

"And freshly made," Old Dad said, examining it closely.

"Maybe Dakota put it there himself," Ricky suggested. "Let's catch up and ask him right now."

But Pete thought that following the tire marks was more important. Old Dad agreed, and the three riders continued their search beside the stream. All at once the tracks turned sharply to the right and stopped at the water's edge.

"The jeep must have crossed here," Pete said. He rode through the shallow water to the other side, but reported no tracks visible there.

Old Dad looked up and down the river. "Maybe those varmints backtracked the truck." He suggested that Pete retrace their steps and look carefully for any place where the vehicle may have turned off. Their search, however, was in vain. "Those thieves must be working magic," Pete said, as he returned to the clearing.

"As long as we're here," Old Dad said, "we'd better rest and water the horses."

Ricky led his mount to the stream. Behind him, several yards from the water's edge, was a huge rock slope which slanted sharply upward. Near the top of it he could see a low overhang, forming a cave.

"Maybe Dakota's hiding up there," Ricky thought to himself. "I'll go take a look."

The huge rock slope did not reach all the way to the ground, but dropped off sharply about five feet above it. Unnoticed by the others, Ricky pulled himself up the little precipice and clambered onto the slope. He had crawled halfway to the top before his brother spotted him.

"Where you going?" Pete called.

"I'll be right down," Ricky answered. He reached the mouth of the cave and crawled in. Warily he stood up. The cave was much larger and darker than he had thought.

Cautiously the boy took a few steps, then froze with fright. Deep within the cave shone two yellowish eyes. Ricky's heart pounded. He began to back away when suddenly a low growl echoed in the black cave.

CHAPTER 10

Hidden Clue

WHEN Ricky heard the growl and saw the gleaming eyes he tried to cry out. His jaw moved up and down but no sounds came forth. Farther back in the cave, glowing dimly, was a larger pair of eyes!

Ricky burst out of the cavern and half ran, half slid down the rocky slope. Breathless, he reached the bottom and raced toward Pete and Old Dad.

"The cave up there!" he cried, turning and pointing toward the top of the slope. "It's full of wild animals!"

Pete and the old cowboy shielded their eyes and looked. As they did, a tawny beast crept out of the cave and bounded down the other side of the hill.

"Loopin' lariats!" Old Dad exclaimed. "You were right, Ricky. That's a mountain lion. Could be the same one I've been hunting."

"But there's another one in the cave," Ricky said emphatically. "It's a million times bigger."

Pete and Old Dad smiled at the disheveled boy, who was now slapping the dust from his Levi's. The seat of his trousers had been worn shiny from the slide along the rocky surface.

"Ow!" Ricky yelped, quickly sticking a finger into his mouth.

"What's the matter?" Pete asked.

"Splinters!" Ricky cried. "How did I get them into my Levi's?"

"Not from sliding down a rock, that's for sure," Pete said with a chuckle.

Meanwhile, Old Dad had taken the lunch Mrs. Blair had packed for them out of his saddle bag. "Time to eat," he announced, seating himself on a rock. But first Ricky plucked the splinter from his finger.

After they ate sandwiches and drank a vacuum bottle of cool milk, the three remounted and started back toward the Tumbling K Ranch.

"We've solved plenty of mysteries," Pete said, "but this one's a dilly. The jeep tracks just disappear, and the antelope thieves vanish."

"It's a trick of some kind," Old Dad declared, "and we have to find out what it is."

"Could the thieves be making the lights on the mountaintop?" Pete asked the old cowboy.

"Why would they be foolish enough to do that?" Old Dad replied. "They wouldn't want people to know where they were."

They rode on silently for a while, puzzling over the lights and the disappearing thieves. After they had reached the valley, Ricky looked into Old Dad's weather-beaten face and remarked, "You ought to know all the good hiding places in these mountains."

The cowboy shook his head. "There's plenty of them I don't know," he said. Reining up his horse, he pointed back along the trail from which they had come. "See that fold up in the hills there? That's the entrance to Rustlers' Canyon. It snakes up the side of the mountain and leads to Secret Valley."

"Crickets!" Pete exclaimed. "That sounds exciting. Were there real rustlers here once?"

"I should say so! Chased them myself. But three of them got away from our posse, and we never did find them."

"You think they had a hide-out in Rustlers' Canyon or Secret Valley?" Ricky asked.

"Maybe," said the cowboy. "And I'll tell you about something else that disappeared into these hills and was never found." As they continued along the valley toward the main highway, Old Dad told the boys about a chest of gold coins said to be hidden in the mountains.

"Stagecoach robbers are supposed to have cached it away," he said, "and nobody's ever found it."

"Yikes!" Ricky exclaimed. "Tell us more about the rustlers."

"They were a hardy lot," the old cowboy went on. "One night, when we were moonlighting, I came across their campfire. Then shots rang out. Those fellows yelled and hollered and frightened my horse. Next thing I knew I was pickin' daisies."

"Old Dad," Pete said with a chuckle, "you'll have to talk Eastern language for us."

The cowboy told them that "moonlighting" meant riding after cattle at night. "Picking daisies" was the expression for a rider who has been thrown from his horse.

As they approached the ranch gate, Old Dad said thoughtfully, "We ought to tell Mr. Blair about seeing Dakota at that marked tree, but let's not mention it in front of the others."

Pete and Ricky agreed. "After all," the older boy said, "it isn't fair to make everybody suspect him if we can't prove he's doing wrong."

When they reached the house, everyone was enjoying cookies and lemonade on the portico. Old Dad and the boys dismounted and told their story.

Learning of the mysterious tire tracks, Mrs. Blair wanted to tell the Elkton police immediately. But her husband disagreed.

"These shenanigans are occurring on the Tumbling K," the rancher said. "If a posse goes climbing through these mountains now, our guests might be endangered."

"I've got it!" Pete exclaimed. "Why don't we all go on a pack trip into the mountains? That way we can look for clues."

Bunky and Gina praised the idea, but their father smiled and shook his head. "Old Dad Callahan is the best camper I know of," he said. "But such a trip might be too dangerous."

Pete looked disappointed and glanced up at the Ruby Mountains. "If only we had more definite clues," he thought to himself. "Then we'd have a better reason for the pack trip."

As he and Old Dad led the horses to the corral, Pete asked, "Where could I find some more information about Secret Valley and Rustlers' Canyon?"

Old Dad opened the corral gate, and the horses trotted inside. He thought the question over for a long time, and then replied, "There aren't too many old-timers left to tell you stories. But there are some books in the library."

"Then that's where we'll look!" Pete declared.

"Oh, Pam!" he shouted and ran toward his sister. Quickly he told her his plan to read about the robbers' hide-out in the Rubies.

"That's fine, Pete," his sister replied. "We girls are going to the library tomorrow morning anyhow." Pam said that Cindy had told them about the tryouts for a western play to be given by local children at the library.

"Cindy is taking us," Pam explained. "I'm sure she won't mind if you boys come too."

After supper that evening, Pete, Ricky, and Old Dad took Mr. Blair aside. They told him about seeing Dakota Dawson standing by the tree marked with an X.

"I'll admit it does look a little suspicious," the rancher said, "but I have confidence in Dakota. As for the X, it might have been a trail marker put there by hunters who wandered onto our property."

Mr. Blair nevertheless promised to observe Dakota in an effort to determine whether he was doing things other than his ranch work.

Next morning Cindy borrowed one of the Tumbling K pickup trucks and drove the Hollisters and the two Blair children to the Elkton library. It was a small red brick building nestled on a shady street one block from the center of town. Cindy led them up the steps, and they trooped inside. The ranch girl walked over to a pretty dark-haired woman seated behind the main desk.

"Miss Fell," she said, "I would like to introduce you to the Hollisters. They're from back East and are out here to solve a mystery."

"Goodness, that sounds exciting," the librarian said, and shook hands with each of them.

Pete asked Miss Fell if he might examine old books about the Ruby Mountains. She led him to a stack and pointed out several well-worn volumes. Pete immediately chose one, seated himself at a table, and began to pore over the old stories.

"Are you having fun in Nevada?" Miss Fell asked, as she returned to the other children.

Little Sue had been looking intently at a large plastic world globe on a stand beside the librarian's desk. When she heard Miss Fell's question, she answered eagerly, "I caught a fish already."

"Really! Where?"

"At the Tumbling K pond." Sue's eyes sparkled as she went on, "And it was *this* big."

The little girl flung her arms wide, but in doing so, she knocked the plastic globe to the floor.

"Oh!" Sue cried with a horrified look. "I—I broke the world!"

As she stopped and tried to pick it up, a small metal plug fell out. Immediately there was a hissing sound. The round sphere started to go flat.

"Oh Sue, look what you've done!" Holly exclaimed.

"I broke the world."

"Don't worry," Miss Fell said, stepping over to the deflated world.

"There's a little plastic tube near the North Pole. We'll just blow some more air into the old world, and it will be all right again."

This remark made the others chuckle.

"Let me blow it up," Bunky volunteered. With several long deep breaths, he had the world back in shape again. Then he fitted the small metal plug securely into the tube. Miss Fell placed the globe back on the stand.

"No harm done," she said, smiling at Sue. Then turning to Cindy, she added, "Are these girls trying for the part of Laurie in our play?"

"I am," Pam said.

"Well, tryouts will be in the children's room in the basement in fifteen minutes."

With Pete still studying the old books, the rest of the children descended the flight of stairs to the basement room. There they found half a dozen girls about Pam's age. Among them was Millie Simpson.

"Ugh!" Ricky declared, but Pam nudged him before he could say more.

At the desk sat a young woman studying a sheaf of papers. Cindy introduced her as Miss Rondo, the assistant librarian.

Miss Rondo explained that the town children were giving a play called *Sweet Laurie from Springtime.*

"Springtime is a little mountain village, and Laurie is the name of the heroine. I want you girls to look over the part." She handed out printed sheets to the candidates and asked the rest of the children to please remain quiet while the prospective Lauries studied.

Upstairs, meanwhile, Pete pulled a thin volume from the stacks. It was titled *Rustlers' Gold*. The subtitle was *Adventures in the Ruby Mountains*.

As Pete read through it, he came to a chapter called "An Unsolved Secret." It told of a chest of gold which had been stolen from a stagecoach on its way to California. One of the robbers had confessed to hiding the loot in Secret Valley. But it had never been found.

"This must be the chest of gold Old Dad mentioned," Pete thought. He was so excited that he hastened to Miss Fell's desk.

"I think I've found what I wanted," the boy said and pointed out the interesting information. "I'll bet there's a hide-out in Secret Valley that nobody knows about to this very day," he declared.

"You may be right, Pete," the librarian replied. "The mountains hold many secrets."

"Crickets, I'm glad I found this book, Miss Fell," Pete said. "It gives me a wonderful clue. I'm going to Secret Valley!" Pete added, as he started toward the stacks to return the old book.

The librarian smiled and remarked, "You may have company, Pete."

Pete looked dumfounded. "Who?"

"A young lad named Terry Bridger," the woman said, "and a man named Dawson."

CHAPTER 11

A Telltale Map

WHEN Pete heard the news, his face became scarlet. Words stuck in his throat.

"Dawson?" he asked feebly.

"Yes. He's a new cowboy. He said he works for Mr. Blair. You must know him."

Pete nodded. "Who is Terry Bridger?"

The librarian said that Terry was an outdoors boy who loved to roam the mountains on his horse. "He lives not far from here," she added. "I'll give you his address."

Pete took the slip of paper she handed him. He looked glum. So the clue he had found had been discovered by two others before him. What was Dawson's interest in Secret Valley? And was Terry Bridger helping the mysterious cowboy in whatever he was up to?

Pete thanked the librarian and asked where Pam had gone. When she told him, he hurried downstairs, entered the children's room quietly, and took a seat at the back.

Up in front Miss Rondo was saying, "Take the speech on page twelve. Laurie is alone in her cabin. She hears a knock on the door. She hurries to open it, thinking it's her father. Instead it's Two-gun Gerald, the bad prospector. Laurie backs up, afraid, and says, 'What do you want? We haven't got the gold here. Please go away! Go away!' "

The librarian added, "The most important thing is not what you say but how you act."

As the girls took turns reading their lines, Pete gazed straight ahead as if in a trance. Would this be the first mystery they failed to solve? Thoughts of Dawson and Terry Bridger riding through the hills at that very moment tormented the boy. He also pondered hard about the problem of the disappearing jeep. Pete was roused from his reverie by Pam's voice.

"We haven't got the gold here!" Pam said pleadingly. "Please go away! Go away!" She shrank back from the imaginary prospector.

Holly giggled and whispered to Ricky, seated beside her. "Pam's the best!"

Miss Rondo felt the same way. Rising from her desk, she said, "Pam, you have won the part of Sweet Laurie."

All of the other girls with the exception of Millie clapped.

"Good for you, Pam!" Gina said.

Pam smiled delightedly, then glanced at Millie. The girl looked downcast and turned her eyes to the floor.

"Who was second best, Miss Rondo?" Pam asked.

"Millie, I would say."

"I don't want the part," Pam said. "I think Millie should have it."

"But why?" the dramatic coach asked in amazement.

"My brothers and sisters and I have a mystery to solve," Pam answered, "so I don't think I'll have time to practice, Miss Rondo."

"Well, in that case," the woman replied, "Millie may have the part."

Millie's face brightened. She walked up to Pam and whispered in her ear, "Thank you so much. I don't know anyone as kind as you."

Just then Pete tapped Pam on the shoulder, saying, "I have bad news." He took her aside and told about the old book which had already been studied by Dawson and Terry Bridger.

"I'm going to look up Terry right away," Pete said. "Tell Mother I'll be back at the ranch later."

After telling Cindy where he was bound, Pete said good-by. "I'm going to take the children back to the ranch now for lunch," the girl said, "and return to the library. I'll meet you here this afternoon and drive you home."

Pete hurried out of the building, studying the piece of paper the librarian had given him. The address was 17 Custer Street. He found it without difficulty. Number 17 was a little white cottage which was set back from the sidewalk in the shade of a tall cottonwood tree.

Pete mounted the front steps and knocked on the screen door. A woman appeared in the dim hallway. Seeing Pete's silhouette, she cried out, "Terry, where have you been?"

Then coming closer, the woman realized her mistake. "Oh, I'm sorry," she apologized. "I thought you were my son. You're about the same size. Sometimes he knocks on the door to tease me."

Pete introduced himself and said, "Mrs. Bridger, I'm looking for Terry myself. Where is he?"

"Oh dear, I wish I knew," Mrs. Bridger replied, opening the door. "Come on in. I'll tell you about him."

Pete entered the neat living room and took a seat. "It might sound strange, Mrs. Bridger," Pete began, "but I'm looking for Terry because of a book in the library. Does your son know a man named Dakota Dawson?"

Mrs. Bridger looked thoughtful for a moment, then shook her head. "No, I've never heard him mention anyone by that name."

"That's good," said Pete, without meaning to.

"Why do you say that?" the boy's mother asked.

Pete grinned. "It's a long story, Mrs. Bridger," he replied. "It's about a mystery."

Mrs. Bridger threw up her hands and made a wry face. "Mysteries and treasures!" she declared. "Terry's head is always full of those ideas. Right now he's looking for hidden gold in Secret Valley."

Pete's heart sank at the news. He thought, "If Terry's camping in the Rubies, perhaps he's been causing the flickering lights which are frightening Millie Simpson." Then Pete said aloud, "When did he leave?"

"About a week ago," the woman replied. "He should be back by now."

"Did he go alone?" Pete asked.

"Goodness, no," Mrs. Bridger went on. "He's with two other friends about his same age."

Suddenly an idea came to Pete. "Maybe I can help find your son," he offered.

"Well, I wish you would," the woman said. "Terry has a good many chores he should be attending to. But how could you find him?"

Pete told of the possibility of a pack trip into the mountains. At this, Mrs. Bridger sighed. "That'll be like looking for a needle in a haystack," she said.

"Do you know the route your son took?" Pete asked.

"He was working on a map," the boy's mother replied, "but he didn't show it to me."

"Perhaps there's a copy of it in his room," Pete said.

"You're welcome to look," offered Mrs. Bridger, rising. "Come. Follow me."

She led the way to a neat room at the rear of the house. The walls were decorated with pennants and several model airplanes hung from the ceiling by wires. In one corner of the room stood a desk. On it were books and magazines and a pile of papers. Mrs. Bridger looked through them. "I can't seem to find any maps here," she said.

"How about the wastebasket?" Pete asked, bending down. Several crumpled scraps of paper lay at the bottom. Pete unfolded them. The first two contained a list of camping supplies. The third was a crude map.

"Look!" Pete said. "This might be it." He spread it out on the table, smoothing the crinkles. In the left-hand corner were the words *Tumbling K.* Pete's eyes followed the line marked "Icy River." This led into "Rustlers' Canyon." "I'll bet that's the route the jeep took," Pete thought to himself.

A dotted line showed the proposed course of the boys' trip. At the far end of the canyon it veered to the left.

"May I keep this?" Pete asked.

"Look, this might be it."

"Of course," said Mrs. Bridger. "And if you find my son, tell him to hurry home. They had supplies for a week and must be running low now."

Before Pete left, Mrs. Bridger invited him to have a sandwich and a glass of milk, which he accepted. After he had finished, he thanked her and hurried back to the library. There he met Cindy. He confided the information he had learned about Terry Bridger and added, "I'd like to get back to the ranch in a hurry and tell your grandfather."

"I won't be going home until five o'clock, Pete," Cindy said. "But I think I can get a ride for you. That's Mr. McCord at the desk. He's a friend of my father's." She hurried over and spoke to the man, who was about to leave. He nodded to Pete.

"Come on," he said. "I'm going past the Tumbling K. I'll give you a lift."

Half an hour later Pete was racing to the corral where Old Dad was shoeing one of the horses. When he had finished, Pete showed him the map.

"Hmm," Old Dad said. "This boy knows the mountains all right. Then he frowned as his stubby finger traced the route which veered sharply from the canyon.

"That's a mean cliff there," Old Dad commented. "The trail is steep and rocky, but it's a short cut to Secret Valley."

Then Pete told the old cowboy all that he had learned. "It looks as if we should take that pack trip right soon," Old Dad remarked, "but we'll have to get Mr. Blair's permission."

At dinner that evening Pete brought up the subject. "Now we have a real clue to go on," he explained. "The book says the gold is in Secret Valley. That means the robbers may have had a hide-out there. If we could find that, maybe we would locate the antelope thieves."

"Let's do it," Ricky cried out. "I'm not afraid of old mountain lions."

Pam, Gina, and Bunky were equally enthusiastic. Bunky begged his father to let them make the trip.

"I may," the rancher said thoughtfully. "In a few days perhaps."

"But why can't we go now, Daddy?" Gina asked.

"Because I have a big surprise for you all," he said, smiling.

Pete, Pam, Gina, and Bunky lingered at the table discussing with Mr. Blair the clues they had found.

"Why would Dakota be studying a book about Secret Valley?" Gina asked her father.

"Lots of cowboys are studious," he replied. "Many of them do a lot of reading."

"Well it seems mighty strange he picked that subject," Bunky added.

Ricky and Holly, meanwhile, strolled toward the corral to watch the horses. As they did, Holly looked down the road which led to the ranch house. A cloud of dust rose in the distance as a cavalcade of horse vans rumbled toward the Tumbling K.

"Look, Ricky!" Holly cried out. "We're being invaded!"

CHAPTER 12

The Sheriff's Posse

To THE astonishment of Ricky and Holly, the dusty caravan continued on through the gate of the Tumbling K.

"Yikes!" Ricky exclaimed. "Let's tell Mr. Blair!" He and Holly raced to the ranch house. They met their host coming out on the porch with the older children. Close behind were the two mothers, Sue, and Cindy. The rancher smiled broadly.

"Mr. Blair!" Ricky cried out. "Are you going to buy all those horses?"

The man laughed and said, "No, Ricky, these are my guests. This is the big surprise I was telling you about."

Just then the lead van stopped and two men stepped out. They were dressed in riding clothes and bright orange shirts. As one of the men turned to wave the other vans to a halt, the onlookers saw four words written in black on the back of his shirt: "Salt Creek Sheriff's Posse."

Excitement filled the air, and the children asked dozens of questions as the newcomers swung down out of the trucks and strode toward them. The man in the lead thrust his right hand toward Mr. Blair, and the two exchanged a firm grip.

"Welcome to the Tumbling K," the rancher said. Then he turned to the Hollisters, who stood open-mouthed, watching the proceedings. "This is my good friend, Rex Hill," Mr. Blair went on. "He's in charge of the Salt Creek Sheriff's Posse. And now," he added, smiling at Ricky's expression, "I'll answer some of your questions."

As Bunky and Gina grinned at their guests' bewilderment, their father told the Hollisters that in the West there are many riding groups which compete against one another. "Actually they are the outgrowth of the sheriff's posse in the old days," Mr. Blair explained.

"That's right," Rex Hill added, putting an arm around Pete and Pam. "We're going to have a shindig tomorrow at the fair grounds in Elkton."

"Whom are you riding against?" Mrs. Hollister asked.

"There are three other good teams," Mr. Hill answered, "the Idaho Rough Riders, the Utah Mounted Patrol, and the Nevada Silver Spurs."

"Gee whiz," Ricky said sadly, "I thought you had come to help catch the bad men."

Hearing this, the other riders who had gathered about laughed. One of them spoke up, a short fellow with bandy legs and a big smile. "I didn't know you had any bad men left in the Rubies, Ken," he said with a chuckle.

"This is Harmonica Mike, ma'am," Rex Hill put in, nodding toward Mrs. Hollister. With a twinkle, he went on, "Mike's a man to have around a campfire."

Mr. Blair explained that the sheriff's posse would exercise their horses at the Tumbling K and that the riders would sleep that night on cots in the bunkhouse. "Then tomorrow they ride into town for the big show," he added.

Pam glanced toward the bunkhouse. Standing beside it was Dakota Dawson. When he saw Pam he quickly turned away, strode to where his horse was tied, mounted, and rode toward the hills.

Pam hastened to Mr. Blair and told him what she had seen. "I think he's afraid of all the sheriff's men," she said.

"I don't think so," the rancher replied. "Dakota has to round up some stray calves I saw on the range this morning."

But Pam was convinced that there was something suspicious about the mysterious cowboy. As the sheriff's posse began to unload the horses from the vans and lead them into the big corral, Pam took Pete aside. "If Dakota had to go after those calves," she said, "why didn't he do it sooner?"

"Maybe he wanted to see the Salt Creek men," Pete replied. "If Dakota *is* the same man we saw hurrying from the sheriff's office, he may know these fellows."

"But if he knows them, why didn't he say hello?" Pam persisted. "I think he's afraid of them."

By the time the horses had been taken care of, the setting sun had dropped below the rim of mountains and a cool evening breeze sprang up.

As the children chatted with the gaily dressed riders, Old Dad came out of the bunkhouse. "Where have you been?" Holly asked, running over to him.

"Getting ready for these fellows," the old cowboy replied. Then he bent down and whispered into her ear, "Do you want to have some fun?"

"Sure. Doing what?"

"Follow me. Bring the rest of the kids, too."

In a few minutes all five Hollisters, along with Bunky and Gina, had followed Old Dad into a clearing near the barbecue pit.

"How would you like to help me make a campfire?" Old Dad asked.

"That's super!" Pete declared. "What shall we do?"

"Gather wood."

The children scattered about like frightened jack rabbits to gather twigs and branches. Pete and Bunky ran to the woodpile and returned with armloads of logs.

"That's fine," said Old Dad, and in a few minutes the small crackling blaze he started had grown to a giant bonfire. Darkness seemed to creep up from the valley, and as it did the men from the sheriff's posse gathered around the campfire. The children's mothers walked over from the house with Cindy, and the light flickered on their happy faces.

All of a sudden, the jolly, reedy tunes of a mouth organ filled the air as Harmonica Mike started to entertain. Soon everyone was singing, "Get Along Little Dogie," and other western songs.

As many feet tapped out the rhythm, Sue, who had been holding her mother's hand, hopped forward and started a little dance of her own.

When the singing ended everyone clapped and Rex Hill stepped forward, lifting Sue up in his arms. "I think we'll adopt you for our mascot," he said. "How about it, boys?"

The Salt Creek Sheriff's Posse cheered and filled the air with cowboy yells.

Then Sue tugged at Mr. Hill's ears, rolled her eyes, and said, "I'll be your mascot if you'll do me a favor."

"What's that?"

"If you'll help us find the bad men after your show tomorrow."

"We'll have to go home tomorrow night," Rex Hill told her. "But we could start late. We'll ride through these hills until it gets dark, and I'll guarantee that we'll find any bad men who are hiding there." Sue gave the man a quick kiss and wriggled down to run to the side of her mother.

Pete, who was standing beside Bunky, said, "That'll be great. With all those fellows on the search, we'll solve this mystery in no time."

After several more songs had been sung and the bonfire had slumped down into a pile of glowing embers, the party broke up.

As Pam started back toward the ranch house, she peered into the darkness at a woman's figure moving toward the thicket.

"Mother, is that you?" Pam called out.

"Mother, is that you?"

"No, here I am, dear," Mrs. Hollister replied. She was walking directly behind the girl, with Mrs. Blair and Cindy.

"Well, who is that woman over there?" Pam asked.

"Where?"

"She just vanished into the woods. I'm sure it was a woman," Pam said.

Hearing the urgency in his sister's voice, Pete hurried to her side. "Do you think someone was spying on us?" he asked.

"Well, it wasn't Cindy or Mrs. Blair or Mother," Pam said.

When Bunky heard what had happened, he ran ahead into the house and returned with a flashlight. But a search through the bushes and trees revealed nothing. Finally he and Pete gave up.

"Maybe it was just a shadow you saw," Cindy suggested as they all went into the house.

But Pam went to bed that night still thinking about the flitting figure.

Everyone was up early the next morning. The Hollisters visited Gina and Bunky's Sunday school. When they returned, they found the Salt Creek Sheriff's Posse mounted to the man and ready to ride into Elkton.

"Good-by, good-by!" The children waved to the orange-shirted riders as they set off.

"Remember, Sue," Rex Hill called, "you're our mascot, and we'll see you at the fair grounds."

Immediately after Sunday dinner, the Blair children got into the family car to drive with their parents to the show at Elkton. The Hollisters were to follow right behind. "Aren't you coming, Old Dad?" Pam asked, as she stepped into the station wagon.

"No, I have to stay here and mind the ranch," he said. "I'll see you later."

When they arrived at the grounds, they made their way to the grandstands, which were filling quickly. There was a flurry of excitement as a voice boomed over the loud-speaker. "First we will introduce the Idaho Roughriders." Just then a man dressed in a red shirt and cowboy hat, and carrying a red and white flag, raced his horse before the stands. He was followed by a long line of red-shirted riders. They rode around in one circle. Then they broke up into two circles. Next they trotted four abreast, then eight abreast. Their maneuvers were precise and snappy.

"Yikes, they're great!" Ricky exclaimed. "I hope the Sheriff's Posse does as well."

The dust had hardly settled from the Idaho Roughriders when the Utah Mounted Patrol took the field. They were dressed in black, with white hats. When they had finished their performance, the Nevada Silver Spurs galloped before the grandstands with thudding hoofs. They were dressed in blue breeches and silver shirts.

The children had been so busy watching the show that they had not paid much attention to one another. What a surprise they had when the Salt Creek Sheriff's Posse paraded gallantly onto the field. They rode in slowly, for on the lead horse sat little Sue Hollister! She was dressed in riding breeches and a tiny orange shirt. In one hand she carried a cowboy hat, which she waved at the crowd.

CHAPTER 13

A Bag of Gold

"THAT's Sue!" Pam exclaimed, hardly able to believe her eyes.

"Mother, you didn't tell us!" Holly reproached, tugging at Mrs. Hollister's hand.

Their mother laughed gaily and said, "Mrs. Blair and I worked far into the night to make that shirt." She added that the riding breeches had been worn by Gina when she was little.

Using their mascot as a pivot, the Salt Creek Sheriff's Posse went into many intricate maneuvers, while the onlookers cheered. When the events were over, Sue rode out of the arena at the head of the procession.

Shortly afterward the loudspeaker announced that the Salt Creek riders had won the competition. The Hollisters and their friends stood up and shouted.

"They were wonderful!" Pam declared.

"I think that Sue helped them to win the prize," was Pete's remark.

They all left the grandstand and made their way through the crowd toward the barn, where the riders were dismounting. Mr. Hill lifted Sue from her horse and said, "I knew we'd win with you as our mascot."

"But don't forget your promise," Sue reminded him, as her family hastened over to her.

"We won't," Rex Hill said. He told them his troop would ride back to the ranch, and then search the Ruby Mountains until it was time for them to put their horses into the vans and depart.

With all the children in the station wagon, Mrs. Hollister drove through Elkton and along the highway which led to the Tumbling K. Then she turned off toward the foothills and soon was driving down the winding road which led to the ranch gate.

But as they approached the house, everyone cried out in dismay. *All the horse vans had been rolled down into the meadow in a terrible jumble!*

"Oh, look what's happened!" Pam cried out.

"Who could have done it?" Gina asked, nearly in tears.

Many of the vans stood upright, but some had fallen on their sides. One had turned completely upside down.

Mr. and Mrs. Blair, driving directly behind them, were equally shocked at the fantastic sight. After pulling up in front of the ranch house, Mr. Blair leaped out of the car, shouting, "Old Dad, where are you? What's happened?"

Everything was silent, and the old cowboy was nowhere to be seen.

"I'll search in the house, Dad," said Bunky, racing off.

"And I'll look in the bunkhouse," Pete volunteered. With Pam at his heels, he dashed inside the building. The cots and bedrolls were neatly in place. On one of

"Old Dad, are you hurt?"

them lay Old Dad. He was bound hand and foot, and a gag was tightly drawn across his mouth.

Pete and Pam ran over to him and quickly unloosed his bonds. "Old Dad, are you hurt?" Pam asked, while Pete ran out to call the others.

The cowboy rubbed the back of his head gingerly. "Just a bump on my head, that's all."

At that moment, the others hastened into the bunkhouse. The old fellow swung his feet over the side of the cot and told them what had happened.

"An old woman rode up on a horse," he said, "and asked if Mr. Blair was home. I said no, but the minute I turned my head, she hit me with something and knocked me out. I reckon she's the one who dragged me in here and tied me up."

"Yikes! She must have been plenty strong!" Ricky said.

"She certainly must have been if she's the one who rolled all the trailers down the embankment," the rancher declared.

"Oh no!" Old Dad groaned. Mr. Blair and Pete helped him to his feet.

"Everything's in a mess," Mr. Blair went on as they left the bunkhouse and walked over to the meadow to survey the damage.

Mrs. Blair, meanwhile, had telephoned the police chief at Elkton, and he promised to come out immediately. He arrived just ahead of the mounted posse, which galloped to the ranch gate. There the riders dismounted and ran to examine the trailers.

The police chief, a broad-shouldered man named Larney, spoke with Mr. Blair and Rex Hill. "This looks like the work of a cruel prankster," the chief said. "Does your outfit have any enemies, Rex?"

"None at all," Mr. Hill replied.

"Then what's the reason for it?" the police chief asked. He turned to the knot of people gathered around him. "Has anybody found any clues?"

"I have one," Pam spoke up. She told about seeing the strange woman in the shadows the night before. "I think she was listening to our plans," Pam said.

"Well I don't think she was a woman at all," Old Dad declared, feeling the lump on his head.

"I get it!" Pete exclaimed. "I'll bet that was a man in disguise."

"You mean the same person who was following us in New York?" Bunky asked, looking questioningly at his father.

"Could be," Pete said, as Mr. Blair nodded soberly.

The chief got a description of the person from Old Dad, then radioed a report to headquarters.

"The local police and the highway patrol will be on the lookout," Larney said. And he added, "Who else was on the premises at the time?"

"Nobody," Old Dad replied. "Everyone was at the fair grounds except Dakota Dawson."

At the mention of the cowboy's name, the chief looked up quickly. "Where was he?"

Mr. Blair said Dakota was rounding up some stray calves.

"When he comes back, I'd like to speak to him," Larney said.

"Goody for the Chief!" Holly whispered to Ricky. "I'll bet Dakota knows something about this."

"And it'll prove we were right, too," Ricky replied, " 'cause I know he's a bad cowboy."

"I hate to disappoint you children," Rex Hill said, "but I don't think we'll be able to ride in the hills this evening. We have to get these trailers in shape to carry our horses back to Salt Creek."

Sue looked disappointed that the promise could not be kept, but the older children understood, and said so.

As all of the menfolk put their shoulders to the task of lifting the overturned vehicles, Bunky said, "Pete, Pam, Gina, come over here." He beckoned them to the side of the corral and whispered, "Those culprits, whoever they are, aren't going to get away with this!"

"Right!" agreed Pete. "Let's make up our own posse."

"Without Old Dad?" Pam asked in a doubtful tone.

"He's too busy helping the other men," Bunky replied. "Let's get our horses. We won't be gone very long."

Ricky, Holly, and Sue, meanwhile, had gone to feed the baby antelope, Prairie Star, who had shown great improvement over the past few days.

The older children saddled up, and, as they rode off, Bunky called to his father, "We're going to scout around a little."

"Where?" his father called back.

Bunky motioned with his arm. "Down near Icy River."

"All right. Be careful."

With Bunky in the lead, the children rode down to the flat. For a while they trotted their horses parallel to the highway, then turned toward the Rubies. In half an hour they came to Icy River, gurgling down from the mountains.

So far they had seen nobody.

"I've got a hunch," Pete said. "Let's look at that tree with the X mark on it."

As they rode slowly beside the river, all four of them kept a sharp lookout, both in the woods around them and on the ground as well.

"If anybody sees fresh horse tracks, holler," Bunky ordered.

The trail now led uphill toward the spot where Pete and Ricky had seen Dakota Dawson standing beside the pine tree. As they neared the little clearing, Pete pointed ahead in the distance to the huge sloping rock formation that Ricky had scrambled down when he saw the mountain lion.

Just then Gina cried out, "Horse tracks! Look!"

Bunky slid out of his saddle and examined the ground. "They're fresh tracks," he said. "We must be careful. Don't make any noise."

He mounted again and led the way, following the hoof prints. They disappeared at the river's edge, beside the clearing.

"We have to be careful," Pete said. "Someone may be hiding on the other side of the stream, observing us."

While Pete and Bunky scanned the woods across the Icy River, Pam and Gina continued on to the tree which the boys had pointed out across the open glade.

"There's the X mark," Gina said.

"But what's that?" Pam asked, pointing.

"Where?"

"There, next to that little rock at the foot of the tree. It looks like a sack."

The two girls dismounted, walked to the tree, and knelt down to examine the small bag. It was made of leather, and a thong was tied around the neck of it.

Pam carefully picked it up. "Oh, it's heavy!" she said.

"Let's see what's in it," Gina suggested.

"Okay, I'll untie it."

Pam unloosed the drawstring and gazed inside the small sack. "It's full of gold!" she gasped.

CHAPTER 14

Girl Detective

"Is IT real gold?" Gina questioned, as Pam let the small yellow nuggets drop through her fingers back into the little bag.

"What else could it be?" Pam asked. She rose and called out, "Pete! Bunky! Come here quick!"

The two boys spurred to the tree and dismounted. When Pam showed them the sack, their mouths dropped open in astonishment. But before they could gather their wits, hoofbeats sounded on the other side of Icy River.

All four children glanced up to see a rider urging his horse into the swirling water. The man was dressed in jodhpurs, a dark shirt, and a peaked cap. Around his neck he wore a red-and-white checkered bandanna. His face looked old and wizened.

"Drop that bag! It belongs to me!" the man shouted, as his Appaloosa horse felt cautiously for safe footing in the rock-strewn shallow river.

The suddenness of this new danger caught the four youngsters by surprise. For several moments they stood and stared at the old man. Then a thought flashed through Pete's mind. Pam had found the gold on Mr. Blair's property. This intruder would have to prove it was his!

"Mount up!" Pete cried to the others, and they ran to their horses, Pam clutching the leather pouch tightly in her right hand.

The children flung themselves into their saddles just as the beautifully marked Appaloosa horse reached their shore.

"Follow me!" Bunky cried. "Giddap! Come on, boy!" he urged his mount.

With a few slaps on the flanks, the children's horses raced off. The intruder, his face contorted with rage, galloped close behind them. Bunky's horse was in the lead. Following him came Pam, then Gina and Pete.

The ranch boy led the mad dash out of the foothills and through the sagebrush of the valley. At first the Appaloosa horse kept close behind the Tumbling K animals. But after ten minutes of furious riding, the Blair horses showed that they had more stamina.

"We're losing him!" Pete cried exultantly, as he glanced back over his shoulder at their wrinkled-faced pursuer.

Halfway to the Tumbling K, the man shook his fist, wheeled the Appaloosa about, and galloped off in the opposite direction.

Now Bunky reined up, and the four continued at a canter.

"Crickets! That fellow nearly scared the daylights out of me," said Pete.

"Same here," Bunky declared. "Do you still have the gold, Pam?"

"Yes, right here," the girl said. Her face was flushed as she held up the leather bag for all to see. "But I nearly dropped it, I was so frightened."

"Where do you suppose he came from?" Pete asked the Blair children as they neared the gate of the Tumbling K.

Bunky shook his head. "I don't know. But did you ever see such a face?"

"Enough to scare a Halloween witch," Pam said.

"He sure looked like a dude with those fancy clothes," Gina said. "Do you really think the gold belonged to him?"

"We'll see," Bunky replied, and added, "It might not really be gold, for all we know."

When the four arrived at the ranch house, supper was over and everyone was worried about them. But when their mothers saw that the children were unharmed, they set out the food they had been keeping hot. As Pam, Gina, Pete, and Bunky ate and told their story, the others listened in amazement.

"Why it sounds like a fairy tale!" Mrs. Hollister declared. "I'm so glad you weren't hurt."

Bunky helped himself to a big baked potato. "I think Pete and I could have handled that fellow, but we didn't want to take any chances."

"By Jiminy," Mr. Blair said, as he examined the contents of the pouch, "this certainly does look like gold. But where did it come from?" He turned to Old Dad, who grinned at the four children with great admiration.

"I've never heard of gold in these mountains. Have you?" he asked the old cowboy.

Old Dad considered a moment. Then he addressed a question to his son, Bronc. "When you were a little maverick," he said, "you took a camping trip one day and found a nugget in one of the streams, didn't you?"

"Yes," the foreman answered. "But I've never heard of any mining around here."

After the four oldest had finished eating, all the children followed the men to the portico.

Bronc Callahan took the sack of nuggets and drove quickly to Elkton, where he knew a man who could assay it.

While he was gone the others discussed the mystery. Suddenly a startled expression came to Pete's face. "Where's Dakota Dawson?"

"He hasn't come back," Mr. Blair said. "I noticed a bedroll on the back of his saddle when he left yesterday. Maybe he'll camp out a night or two more."

"Yup," Old Dad said. "Cowboys like to sleep under the stars." With a note of seriousness, he added, "If this really is gold, we ought to start our trip day after tomorrow."

"Why not tomorrow?" Pete asked.

"We need supplies," Old Dad said, "such as a new lizard scorcher."

"A lizard scorcher?" Holly said. "What's that?"

At this Mr. Blair laughed and explained that a lizard scorcher was Western slang for a portable stove which could be carried on a pack mule.

"That's right," Old Dad continued. "We need a couple of mules and then, let's see—who's gonna be doughbelly?"

"Ha, ha, ha!" Ricky burst out. Holly joined him in laughing until her sides ached. "What funny kind of a thing is a doughbelly?" she finally gasped.

"Now see here, don't make fun of the cook," Old Dad said. "That's the most important person on a camping trip."

Mr. Blair chuckled and told the Eastern youngsters that "doughbelly" was the nickname given to a cook, because he often got the front of himself splattered with flour and dough.

"Yikes! That's what I want to be!" Ricky declared. "Doughbelly Ricky."

An hour later Bronc Callahan returned from Elkton. His face wreathed in a king-sized smile, Bronc strode into the living room, where the others were still discussing the mystery.

"You kids hit the jackpot all right. It *is* gold," he said, holding up the bag.

"Yowee!" Bunky cried out.

"Did you find out anything about the funny little old man?" Pete asked Bronc.

The cowboy said he had dropped by to see the police chief, but Larney knew of nobody in Elkton by that description.

"We'll have to do more sleuthing on that tomorrow," Pam suggested.

Tired and happy from their day of adventure, the children went to bed later than usual, but rose when the sun turned the eastern sky into a panorama of pink.

"It *is* gold!"

Old Dad poked his head in the door even before the youngsters had finished breakfast. "Come on, my buckaroos," he said. "We have some shopping to do."

"And a couple of mules to rent," Mr. Blair reminded him.

"Where can we get them?" Pete asked, as he finished a stack of pancakes. Bunky told them that there was a livery stable in Elkton. Tut Primrose, the proprietor, usually had a few mules to hire.

Mrs. Hollister gave Cindy permission to drive the station wagon into Elkton. "I'll watch over Sue," she promised as Old Dad and the seven children set off.

"Tell you what we'll do," Old Dad said, as he stepped spryly from the station wagon in front of the general store. "Pete, Ricky, Bunky, and I will tend to the lizard scorcher and the rest of the supplies. Cindy, you and the girls can hire the mules."

"Okay, Grandpa," Cindy agreed, and set off with the Hollister girls and Gina. They went down the street, turned the corner, and walked two blocks until they came to a big barn. Over its wide-open doors was the sign, Primrose's Livery.

A man stepped out to meet them. He was tall and lean, and wore a floppy felt hat. When he spoke the Adam's apple in his long neck bobbed up and down. Sue was fascinated by it.

"Howdy, Cindy," Tut Primrose said, lifting his hat slightly. "Are you taking your Sunday school class on a picnic?"

"No, we're going on a camping trip in the Rubies and need two pack mules," Cindy told him. She introduced Pam, Holly, and Sue.

"They're detectives from Shoreham," Gina said proudly.

Tut Primrose blinked. "Junior detectives, eh? Well, I could use a good detective."

"Did you lose something?" Pam inquired.

"That's for sure," the livery man said, "and even the local police can't find it."

"Can't find what?" Holly asked.

"My Appaloosa horse!" Tut replied, frowning.

"An Appaloosa!" Pam said, catching her breath. "Did you see a little old man around here wearing riding breeches and a red and white bandanna?"

"Yup," Tut answered. "He's the one I rented the animal to. Have you seen him?"

"We saw him *and* your horse," Gina replied.

Pam did not want to reveal too much of their information. But she told enough to convince Tut Primrose that the man was in the area.

"Well, if you see him again," Tut said, "tell him I'm holding his suitcase until I get my horse."

The girls exchanged startled glances—all but Sue, who kept watching Tut's Adam's apple.

"He left a bag here?" Cindy's voice rang with excitement.

Tut pointed to one of the stalls inside the barn. Beside it lay a brown suitcase. Pam hurried over to look at it. "If we open it," she said, "we may find a clue to the owner's whereabouts."

Tut chuckled and stroked his stubbly beard. "I guess you are a lady detective at that," he said, and reached for the bag.

The two hasps were not locked. Tut snapped them open. As he lifted the lid, the girls cried out in surprise.

CHAPTER 15

Summer Snowballs

INSIDE the suitcase were several wigs, a woman's dress, and a theatrical make-up kit. But there was nothing to indicate the name or address of their owner.

"That fellow must be an actor," the livery man said as he snapped the bag shut again.

Instantly Pam and Gina had the same thought: Could this person be the one who had followed the Blairs in New York, using first one disguise and then another?

"Maybe he's the man who dropped the blond wig in front of our house," Holly suggested.

"Well, he's certainly the one who chased us on the Appaloosa," Pam said. "But he might not have been old at all. He may have used make-up to look so wrinkled," she declared.

"And he was probably the 'woman' who hit Old Dad on the head and overturned the horse trailers," Gina added. "And the one Pam saw after the bonfire."

The girls talked excitedly about the discovery. Then Cindy thanked Tut Primrose for letting them see the suitcase. "It provides us with a good clue," she said, "and I hope we'll be able to find your Appaloosa now."

"Glad to help," came the reply. "Now about those mules, I've got two hefty working critters you may have. Come in the back and look 'em over."

The mules, standing quietly in their stalls, twitched their ears and turned their heads to look at the girls.

"They'll do," Cindy said. "Can you deliver them to the Tumbling K right away?"

Tut said he would put the mules in his horse van and set out for the ranch within the hour. His callers thanked him and started back toward the place where they had parked the station wagon.

Little Sue, who had not said a word, tugged Cindy's hand and looked up into her face. "Isn't it too bad about Mr. Primrose?" she said. "He must have swallowed bubble gum, and it got stuck in his throat."

The girls laughed, and by the time they had explained that the lump was the livery man's Adam's apple, they had reached their car. Pete, Ricky, Bunky, and Old Dad were pushing the final box of supplies over the tail gate.

"All set?" the old cowboy asked.

"We got the mules," Cindy reported.

"And a scee-rumptious clue!" Gina announced. When Pam quickly told about the missing Appaloosa and the suitcase full of disguises, Pete could hardly wait to start back to the Tumbling K.

"Let's leave early in the morning, Old Dad," he coaxed as Cindy guided the station wagon through town and onto the highway.

"All right. You can select your horses right after lunch."

When Cindy pulled up in front of the ranch house the hungry youngsters were greeted by the tempting aroma of juicy grilled hamburgers. As the boys helped unload the supplies, the girls raced around the back of the house to find their mothers setting out a picnic. Much to their surprise, they saw that Millie Simpson was helping.

"You're just in time," Mrs. Blair said. "Millie came for her riding lesson, and I asked her to stay."

"She's been a real helper," Mrs. Hollister said with a smile for Millie.

Ricky, Pete, and Bunky finished carrying the supplies into the bunkhouse and hastened to join the girls at the picnic table.

"Yikes!" Ricky said in a muffled voice to Pete. "Millie's going to serve us. What do you make of that?"

"She's learning how to get along with people, I guess," Pete decided. Just then Millie set a paper plate with a hamburger and potato chips in front of him and smiled.

"Thanks!" the boy said with a grin.

After a jolly lunch, Millie beckoned to Pam, and the two girls moved off into the shade of the big cottonwood tree.

"I'm sorry I was mean to you, Pam," Millie apologized. "I—I spilled my soda on purpose."

"Forget about it," Pam replied. "We're good friends now, aren't we?"

"I would like to be," Millie replied. "And I'm not going to be a 'fraidy cat from now on!"

That afternoon the young riders selected their mounts for the following day's adventure. Seeing Millie watching at the corral gate, Pam and Gina invited her on the camping trip.

"Is Sue going too?" Millie asked.

"No, she's too small," Pam said. "And besides, someone must take care of Prairie Star."

"Then I'll stay home and keep Sue company," Millie said, "if I may." Mrs. Blair was happy to make arrangements to have Millie Simpson remain at the ranch, and Sue also was delighted with the idea.

Later that evening, Old Dad sauntered up to the porch just before the children's bedtime. "Everything's all set," he announced. "Mules and the supplies are ready. We'll start at sunup."

True to his word, Old Dad roused everyone early. By the time the sun was standing on the rim of the mountains, the caravan was lined up and ready to go.

Old Dad turned in his saddle to survey the rest of the column. Directly behind him came Holly, then Ricky, Pam, Gina, Bunky, Pete, and Cindy. The two mules, packed high with camping gear, served as the caboose.

With waving hats and shouts of good-by, the party set off through the ranch gates with a clatter of hoofs.

They went, as they had before, down into the valley, across it, and up the trail beside the Icy River. Their first stop was at the marked tree. There everybody dismounted to water the horses, and the children looked about for more possible clues to the strange rider who had chased them.

"Mount up!" Old Dad ordered, and they all quickly moved to obey.

Now the climb became steeper. As they followed the river it grew narrower and more turbulent. The horses' breathing was labored, and they walked slower.

"We're pretty high," Cindy called out. She pointed to the aspen trees, which now grew more abundantly than the pines.

At noontime the riders stopped at a tiny mountain meadow. There they ate the sandwiches and drank the chilled chocolate milk which Mrs. Blair had put in vacuum bottles.

"I've got a real surprise for you up ahead," Old Dad said. "Finish your vittles, and we'll go see it."

"What is it?" asked Holly as she licked a crumb from her chin. But Old Dad only winked. Soon the campers remounted and headed up a narrow ravine toward the summit of the mountain.

When they reached the top and started down the other side, Old Dad pointed to the base of a jagged peak. Nearby, at the foot of its northern slope, lay a blanket of grayish white.

"There's your surprise!" Old Dad said.

"What is it?" Ricky asked.

"Go over and see for yourself."

Ricky quickly rode his horse to the edge of the whitish-looking stuff. He dismounted and touched it.

"It's snow!" Ricky cried out to the others. "Snow in June! I can't believe it."

Bunky, Gina, and Cindy had known what the surprise was, but nevertheless dismounted and joined the Hollisters as they raced to the snowbank.

Old Dad explained that nights were very cold on top of the mountains. This snow, which had fallen in the late spring, had been partially shielded from the sun and thus had not been melted. "This patch stays all summer long," he told the surprised Easterners.

Having thrown all the snowballs he wanted to, Ricky now trudged knee-deep in the drift toward the base of the peak.

"Come on back!" Pam called out. "We're going to leave now."

"Hey wait! Look at this!" Ricky cried. He pointed into the snow and the others hurried to his side.

"Crickets! Footprints!" Pete exclaimed.

"And look, somebody's been scooping up the snow just like us," Pam said, observing the marks in the smooth surface.

"Maybe Terry Bridger and his pals were here," Pete said.

"Or the bad guys," Ricky hastened to add.

After another hour Old Dad said, "The horses have had enough climbing now. We'll make a couple of lean-tos for the night."

Busily the campers began to cut poles and branches. The sun had nearly set by the time they finished the two shelters: one for the girls, the other for the boys and Old Dad. Then Pete and Bunky unpacked the lizard

"Snow in June!"

scorcher. Soon steaks and potatoes were frying on the portable stove.

"This is great!" Pete said with a sigh of content as he finished his meal. "I love camping out!"

"Do you think we'll catch the bad men tomorrow?" Holly asked as they readied their sleeping bags.

"We'll be in the deep woods by then," Old Dad said. "That may be where they're hiding."

The air suddenly grew cold as darkness engulfed the mountaintop. The stars shone brilliantly overhead, and Pete gazed up at them through the leafy covering of the lean-to. Soon all the youngsters were asleep.

Bunky, lying next to Pete, stirred in the middle of the night, then sat upright. He shook Pete and whispered, "I hear something prowling."

Pete, too, sat up and rubbed his eyes. He strained to look into the darkness but could see nothing. Then he heard a rustling sound which made his scalp tingle with fright.

CHAPTER 16

Danger From Above

THE rustling sound was followed by the crack of a snapping twig. Pete wriggled out of his sleeping bag and roused Old Dad, who was snoring gently.

"Wake up!" Pete whispered, shaking the cowboy's shoulder. "There's a prowler around here!"

Old Dad grabbed a flashlight, and as he did another one winked on in the girls' lean-to.

"Is that you walking around, Grandpa?" Cindy's voice came through the darkness.

By this time everyone was aroused. They dressed hurriedly and searched around their camp site.

"I don't see a thing," Pete said.

"Maybe it was a deer or a bear," Cindy suggested.

Gina shivered a little and said, "Or that mean little man who chased us. He could have been spying."

The boys checked the horses and mules, picketed nearby. The animals had not been disturbed.

When Old Dad saw Ricky and Holly rubbing their eyes sleepily, he said, "Let's hit the sack again, children. Everything seems to be safe." The rest of the night passed without incident.

In the morning, after a hearty breakfast, the pack train continued on through the deep forest. After a while

Old Dad led the party into a high-walled chasm with rocky sides glinting in the morning sun. High above, two eagles soared in the cloudless blue sky. The cowboy turned to Holly riding behind him. "This is Rustlers' Canyon," he said, and she passed the word back.

Now the clattering of the horses' hoofs grew louder as they strained upward over the stony trail beside the Icy River. Now and then the horseshoes struck sparks on the flinty rocks. All the while the youngsters looked about with keen eyes but could see no sign of any other persons.

When the sun was almost directly overhead, the riders topped a barren ridge and looked down the other side on a tiny azure lake.

"Oh, how beautiful!" Pam exclaimed.

"It looks like a gem," Cindy remarked, as the younger children oh-ed and ah-ed at the inspiring sight.

"I'll bet it's a crater lake," Pete guessed.

"You're right," said Old Dad. "This was once a volcano."

"Oh, shucks," Ricky said. "We got here a little too late to see it working."

The old cowboy chuckled. "But not too late to catch a mess of fish for lunch, Ricky," he said. Picking the trail carefully, the campers descended to the shore of the lake, which was fringed by sparse growths of pine and aspen. Pete was surprised to learn that neither Bunky nor Gina had ever seen the spot before and were just as thrilled as the Hollisters. They untied their fishing tackle from the pack animals and hastened to the water's edge.

"What are you using for bait?" Pete asked Bunky.

"Artificial flies."

When Bunky's line hit the water, there was a sudden swirl and splash.

"Yikes! He's got one already!" Ricky cried out.

Bunky landed a plump, wriggly trout. He had no sooner removed the hook, when Pete got a strike.

"Crickets, the lake must be alive with fish!" Pete declared.

Old Dad told the children he had led them here with a purpose. "Terry Bridger and his friends might have come this way for some good fishing," he explained. "I wouldn't be surprised if they're still up here somewhere."

In ten minutes the children had caught enough fish for an ample lunch. The boys cleaned the catch, and the girls fried them over the lizard scorcher that Old Dad had quickly set up.

"Where to next, Grandpa?" asked Cindy as they swung into their saddles.

The old cowboy pointed across the lake to a sharp peak rising from the jagged rim of the crater. "I think that's where the flickering lights are coming from," he said. "We'll skirt around this lake and camp over there tonight."

Riding alongside Old Dad, Pete and Bunky helped to pick a trail around the inner slope of the ancient volcano. The way was strewn with boulders, which the cowboy said had fallen down from the craggy rim over the centuries past.

"Jeepers!" Bunky said. "Wouldn't this be a good place for villains to hide out?"

"And that's exactly what they did in the old days," the cowboy replied. Then he pointed high up to their left. "Secret Valley lies over there on the other side of the crater. Some folks think it's even wilder than this old volcano."

This remark caused Pete to glance up at the rugged crags. "What a fine place for an ambush," he thought. In the fleeting second that Pete's eyes rose to the rim, he thought he saw something move. "Old Dad, look!" he cried out. A boulder about three times as big as a basketball detached itself from an outcropping rock and started to tumble down the slope. It skittered and bounced from rock to rock, hitting other stones into movement. The campers watched, fascinated.

"Rock slide!" Old Dad shouted. "Get back! Get back!" he ordered as he wheeled his horse.

Cindy spurred her mount and forced the mules about. As she did, the column retreated single file. Could they make it in time, Pete wondered as he glanced up at the thundering rocks. With booming, cracking sounds the whole side of the crater seemed to be roaring down upon them.

"Hurry, hurry!" Gina screamed.

Old Dad, now at the end of the line, urged Pete's and Bunky's horses on ahead of him with loud cowboy whoops. Holly's mount stumbled momentarily, but regained its footing as the girl clung tightly to the animal's neck.

Pete gave one last backward glance. The tumbling rocks might miss them, but only by a few feet. His gaze flashed to the top of the rim. What he saw there made

"Rock slide, get back!"

his face flush red with anger. The silhouette of a horse and rider paused briefly for a moment, then disappeared down the far side of the crater.

Now, in addition to the thunderous din, the air was filled with particles of sand and rock dust. The avalanche rolled past, so close that a small stone hit the flank of Old Dad's horse. The injured animal let out a terrified whinny, sunfished to a nearly vertical position, then bucked for a few moments. But Old Dad remained in the saddle and soon had his horse under control.

"It's past!" Pam said fervently. "And we're safe!"

Now the riders halted and gazed briefly down the slope toward the lake. The boulders skipped, jumped, and bounded in great arcs, finally hitting the water with great geyser splashes.

As the dust drifted off, Pete said, "Old Dad, I think this rock slide was started on purpose." His companions were startled to hear of the lone rider Pete had spied.

"But who could have known we were here?" Gina asked, puzzled.

"Maybe we're being followed," Pam suggested. "Remember there was someone prowling around our camp last night."

"Starting a rock slide is a terrible thing to do!" Cindy said.

Her grandfather agreed, and declared, "That settles it. We're going to turn back right now. This trip is too dangerous for youngsters."

The Hollisters exchanged looks of disappointment with their companions. After a few moments of silence,

Pete spoke out. "That's just what that rider expects us to do. If we go back, he wins. Can't we just go on until night? If you still think it's too dangerous by that time, then we can turn back."

Pete's fervent plea had its effect upon the white-haired cowboy.

"I admire your courage," he said. "Let's take a vote on it."

"All right," Pete agreed. "All in favor of going on say 'Aye.'"

"Aye!" everyone shouted. Old Dad grinned until his eyes crinkled, and without another word he turned his horse and started back. The riders picked their way cautiously over the rock-strewn hillside. By the time evening had come, they had almost reached their destination.

Riding ahead, Pete and Pam worked their way to the base of the peak to select a camp site. They located a grassy clearing, sheltered from the high crag by a thicket of piñon and juniper bushes.

"We'll sleep under the stars tonight," Old Dad said. "Cindy, you look after the girls."

"And I'll be her assistant," Pam added, smiling.

Pete helped the cowboy unpack the lizard scorcher and started a fire in it, while Gina and Bunky, along with Ricky and Holly, led the horses to a small trickling stream nearby.

Then the girls cooked beans and bacon, while Old Dad mixed a batter which he made into what he called "cowboy biscuits." Everyone agreed that they tasted delicious, especially after a hard day's ride.

When they had finished eating, Old Dad pointed to the top of the peak and said, "This is the highest point on the ridge. I've seen lights flickering up there. We'll watch for them tonight."

The sudden chill after the sun had set caused everyone to climb into bedrolls in order to keep warm. Then, as if by magic, the stars appeared like brilliant gems in the velvet black dome of the sky.

Leaning on their elbows, the campers watched the mountaintop. But Ricky and Holly could not hold sleep back, and their drowsy heads finally nestled in their sleeping sacks.

The others kept watching. Their patience was rewarded an hour later when Gina suddenly exclaimed, "There! I saw something flicker!"

"Where?" Pete asked eagerly.

The girl pointed. "I don't think it's a star," she said. "Do you see it, Pam?"

"It's a light all right," came the reply. Then the others saw it clearly.

"Sizzling lizards!" Old Dad exclaimed. "Somebody's up there. That's for sure."

"Let's get him!" Pete declared, wriggling out of his sack.

The cowboy told them that they must be very careful. "Pete and Bunky and I will tackle him," he went on. "You girls stay here and mind the camp." He turned to Pete and said, "Bring that lariat from my saddle, will you, son?" Pete did as he was asked.

Then together the three started to climb the peak on foot. As they made their way upwards, the flickering lights grew brighter and brighter.

Finally Old Dad and the two boys arrived at the very top of the peak. At the base of a huge rock, they saw a flickering campfire. Three dim figures were hunkered about it. From the distance the stealthy climbers could not determine who the campers were.

"Shall we try to capture them?" Bunky whispered. "Do you think they'll be too strong for us?"

"Let's chance it anyhow," Pete said quietly with determination in his voice.

"Maybe we could trick 'em," Old Dad suggested. "They don't know we're here. If we run up howling like Indians, they may scatter. Then we can catch them one at a time."

At once they dropped to their hands and knees, and crept silently toward the campfire.

Old Dad whispered to the boys, "When I count three, jump up and make the craziest noises you know how."

With every muscle tense, the trio crawled a few more feet.

"One, two," Old Dad whispered, *three!*"

They jumped up, yelling like Indians on the warpath, and dashed toward the three figures seated around the fire.

As Old Dad had anticipated, the startled campers dashed for cover. One of them tripped over a stone. In a flash, Pete and Bunky flung themselves on the prone figure and held on tightly.

"Good work!" Old Dad declared, and shone a flashlight on their prisoner.

"Crickets!" Pete exclaimed, looking into the frightened face. "He's a boy!"

"What's your name, lad?" Old Dad demanded.

"Terry Bridger," came the reply.

CHAPTER 17

An Amazing Discovery

"TERRY Bridger!" Pete exclaimed. "Your mother has been looking for you!"

"She has?" The boy sounded bewildered. "Aren't you the fellows who have been after us?"

"What do you mean?" Bunky asked as Terry rose to his feet and brushed himself off.

Terry still looked suspiciously at the boys and Old Dad. "Before I tell you anything," he said, "who are you?"

After introductions had been made, Terry breathed a sigh of relief. "Jiminy," he said, "I thought we were done for." Terry put two fingers into his mouth and gave three sharp whistles. In a few moments two other boys crept out of the shadows and approached cautiously.

"All right, come on. Don't be afraid. They're friends," Terry called. His two companions hastened to his side. Terry said they were Hal Stone and Ron Gibbs.

"We headed for home two days ago," Terry explained, "but every time we started down Rustlers' Canyon somebody chased us."

"Perhaps you'd better tell us about your trip from the beginning," Old Dad suggested, seating himself on a log beside the campfire.

The three boys, now at ease, told how they had followed the trail beside Icy River and reached the hidden snowbank. There, like the Tumbling K riders, they had stopped to throw snowballs.

"We saw your tracks," said Bunky.

After that, Terry went on, they had ridden to the end of Rustlers' Canyon, where they had taken the short cut to Secret Valley.

"Did you negotiate the cliff?" the old cowboy asked.

"We barely made it," Ron Gibbs replied. "The horses slipped and skidded, so we didn't come back that way."

"When we reached Secret Valley," Terry said, "we searched for the hidden gold, but couldn't find it."

"Did you see anybody else there—a lonesome cowboy, perhaps?" Bunky asked.

"Not a soul," Hal Stone answered. "It wasn't until we left the valley that we had any trouble."

After they had camped by the lake and fished for several days, Terry and his friends had started back down through Rustlers' Canyon.

"A cowboy chased us and scared the wits out of us," Terry said. "We hid behind the boulders near the lake until dark." He said they had started down the canyon again the following day, but when they reached a little muddy stream which emptied into Icy River, they were chased again.

"Was it an old man with a wrinkled face and riding an Appaloosa?" Pete asked.

"No, it was a short, stocky cowboy," Hal replied. "And he was all splattered with mud."

"Then why didn't you go home some other way?" Bunky asked.

"Well, we moved up here because we thought there was a way down behind this peak," Terry replied. "But there isn't."

"We were just trying to figure out what to do when you surprised us," Hal added.

Old Dad said that the mountains in some places were well nigh impassable, but that he knew of a route south of Rustlers' Canyon which would take them safely back to Elkton. By the light of the fire, Old Dad drew a crude map in the dust with a twig, saying, "That's the trail you take, boys."

After Terry had thanked the cowboy, Pete asked, "Were you the ones making the flickering lights on the mountain?"

"No, not us," Ron answered. "We've seen those lights, too. Jiminy, they're pretty mysterious!"

"Why don't we all return to Elkton together?" Hal suggested hopefully. "Our horses are tied over yonder. We could start back in the morning."

"We were going to go to Secret Valley," Pete said. "But, from what you say, I think the bad men are in Rustlers' Canyon."

"That's right," Old Dad agreed.

"We'd better go back there," Pete said.

"And get chased?" Hal asked anxiously.

"I hope so," Bunky declared. "We'd like to catch whoever's prowling around."

It was agreed that Old Dad, Pete, and Bunky would go back to their camp at the base of the peak. Terry and his friends were to set off at daybreak and return to Elkton. The cowboy instructed them to notify the police chief about the mountain prowlers and ask him to send aid to the Tumbling K campers at once.

According to plan, Terry, Hal, and Ron descended from the peak the following morning. They passed the Hollisters and their friends who were just breaking camp. Waving good-by, they headed their horses in the southerly direction that Old Dad had indicated.

"Good luck!" Terry called back. "And don't get into any trouble!"

"We'll try not to!" Pete answered. "Don't forget to send help as soon as you can."

Cindy and the girls had tidied their bedrolls and were ready to set off a few minutes before the boys had doused the fire and packed the lizard scorcher on one of the mules.

"We can't dawdle on the way back," Old Dad said as they mounted. "Holly, Ricky, are you ready for a fast ride?"

"Yippy-yi-ay!" Holly sang out.

"Hurray for the Tumbling K Posse!" Ricky shouted, and with a clippity-clop the pack train started to retrace its steps. The riders worked their way around the lake, climbed the stony slope up to the rim of the crater, and went over the pass. After a quick lunch, they started the steep descent through Rustlers' Canyon, where the Icy River gurgled along beside them.

"Terry gave us a great clue," Pete told Pam. "One of the cowboys who chased him was mud-splattered. So maybe they have a hide-out near the muddy creek he mentioned."

"But the cowboy who chased Terry didn't look a bit like that little old man who came after us," his sister replied.

"I know," Pete said. "But they could all belong to one gang."

The canyon twisted and turned, sometimes wide and sometimes narrow, between high rocky cliffs.

"Watch for that muddy little stream that Terry talked about," Old Dad cautioned his riders. "We should be close to it by now."

"I think I see it!" said Pam, after they had ridden a quarter of a mile farther to where the canyon widened. She pointed off to the right of the trail, where a small brook bubbled among the rocks. It disappeared for a hundred yards. Then it churned its way again to the surface on the other side of the riders and emptied into Icy River.

"Good for you!" Cindy said. "You have sharp eyes, Pam."

All the riders turned their horses to the right, meanwhile keeping a sharp lookout for the cowboys who had chased Terry and his friends. But no one could be seen among the scrubby trees and brush which covered the foot of the cliff.

Soon they stopped beside the gurgling brook. Instead of being a clear mountain stream, as many others were, this one was a muddy brown color.

"Perhaps it runs through a sandy gully on the other side of that cliff," Pete said. He pointed up the sloping floor of the canyon to a rock wall. "Come on," he urged. "Let's see where this stream comes from."

Old Dad cautioned them all to be quiet so they would not arouse anyone who might be stationed as a lookout.

He instructed his charges to ride their horses in the middle of the stream to avoid leaving any hoof prints.

Then Old Dad took the lead. As his horse climbed the slope, it suddenly slipped on the wet stones. With a terrifying thud, the animal fell on its side, pinning the white-haired cowboy underneath. The riders exclaimed in alarm.

"Grandpa, are you all right?" Cindy called as she leaped from her horse and ran to his aid.

The others quickly followed. They found the old cowboy wincing with pain and the horse struggling to get to his feet.

"Is your leg broken?' Pete asked as they led the cowboy to a rock, where he sat down.

"No, I'm all right," said Old Dad, grimacing with pain. "Just a little bruised and shook up, I reckon."

"We'll get you home as quickly as possible," Pam promised, "after you've rested for a little while."

Old Dad protested. "Let Pete see where this stream comes from first," he said. Then he added in a low voice, "Those villains may be spying on us this very minute."

Leaving Old Dad with Ricky and Holly, Pete, Bunky, and the three older girls worked their way up the muddy stream on foot. Finally they came to the rock wall. The stream bubbled out from an opening in the rocks about five feet high and three feet wide.

"Crickets! That's a deep cut in the rocks," Pete said. "Do you suppose it leads anywhere, Bunky?"

"Only one way to find out," he replied firmly.

"But maybe we ought not to leave Old Dad," Cindy said.

"And Ricky and Holly," Pam added.

Looking downstream, they could see the younger Hollisters bathing Old Dad's face with a damp kerchief.

"I guess they're safe enough," Pete said. "Let's go."

Taking the lead, Pete went through the crevice into a dark passage. It took a sharp jog left away from the stream bed. After Pete had felt his way a dozen paces, he whistled in surprise and turned to the others.

"Would you look at this!" he declared. He entered a vault as large as a room. It was faintly lighted by a crack in the ceiling through which he could see blue sky.

One by one, the others stepped into the chamber. As their eyes became accustomed to the dim light, the young explorers were dumfounded at what they saw. Stacked all about the floor of the room were cases of food, odd bits of clothing, picks and shovels.

"We've found the gang's hide-out!" Bunky exulted.

"Look!" Pam whispered. "See what I found!" She held up a sombrero.

"Crickets! That's an old one," Pete said. "It's Spanish style."

"Nobody wears those any more," Cindy remarked.

Pete snapped his fingers. "I'll bet it belonged to one of those old rustlers the posse couldn't find," he said excitedly.

"And this must have been their secret hide-out!" Pam added quickly.

Gina looked around uneasily. "I'd like to know where the gang is that uses it now."

"There's an exit on the other side," Pete said, pointing. "That may give us the answer." With heart pounding, he tiptoed across the stone floor of the cave.

In the opposite wall was another huge crack. Through it, Pete could see dim light. Beckoning the others to follow, he made his way cautiously through the narrow exit, then stopped suddenly.

Pete was speechless. Before him was a tiny box canyon several hundred yards across. On the near side was a wire pen. In it were a dozen small antelopes!

By now Pete was shaking with excitement. He turned and whispered to the others, "Look at this! Don't make any noise."

Small gasps came from the girls as they surveyed the hide-out. The rimrock wall of the little canyon was neatly camouflaged by nature. Small trees and bushes grew from rocky crevices.

"You couldn't spot this even from an airplane," Bunky declared softly.

In the stillness the children listened intently. One of the baby antelopes bleated. Then from across the box canyon came the angry sound of a man's voice.

"You were stupid, Murch, plain stupid!" The words bounced against the rock walls and echoed.

"Don't blame me!" came the reply. "I was about to pick up that gold when the kids came along. I hid so they wouldn't see me."

As a pickup man you're through," came another voice. "It'll take us two weeks to pan that much gold again."

"There—there must be a gold mine right here in the canyon!" Pete stammered.

"I'll go back and get Old Dad," Gina whispered, and slipped quietly back to the rocky crevice.

"Look at this!"

Now the men's voices became muffled in snarled accusations.

"Murch!" Pam exclaimed softly. "He's the one who stole Mother's wallet at the motel."

"Now I understand," Pete said quietly. "He tried to keep us from coming to Nevada."

Just then Murch's voice shrilled out angrily: "What do you mean 'phony disguises?' I did a wonderful job! When I hounded the Blairs in New York, I was four different people. And in Shoreham I was one more, a blond.

"Also remember," Murch added bitterly, "after I got on to the Hollisters' plans through that Brill kid, I gave them plenty of trouble."

"They got here all the same," grumbled a deep voice.

"I've even been an old woman and an old man for you," Murch continued.

"We were right then," Pam whispered to Cindy. "It was all the same person."

Now the mystery began to unfold in Pam's mind. These men had found a gold mine on Tumbling K property. They were trying to work it without Mr. Blair's knowledge or consent.

Just then Old Dad came limping through the narrow defile with Ricky and Holly at his heels. The cowboy's eyes grew wide when he saw the secret hide-out.

"Old Dad," Pete said, "I must have a better look at those men."

"Let well enough alone, son," Old Dad replied. "We'll hurry back and notify the authorities."

"But I have to see if one of them is Dakota Dawson!" Pete whispered. He and Bunky flattened themselves on the ground and wriggled to a small rise of ground. They peeked over it. There in a shallow depression stood four men, shoveling loose gravel into sluicing pans.

One of them, dressed like a cowboy, was tall and broad-shouldered. Another was short and stocky. The third, little and wiry, wore jodhpurs, a red-and-white checkered bandanna, and a peaked cap. But he no longer had the face of an old man. His cheeks were smooth, and he had a sharp look in his eyes. Pete recognized him now as Murch. Next he glanced quickly at the fourth digger. The fellow was fat and had a sandy mustache. *Not one of them was Dakota Dawson!*

After Pete had studied the men long enough, he motioned to his chum to retreat. But as Bunky inched his way backward, his hand pushed a small stone. It rolled down the incline, and in the stillness of the box canyon the pebble sounded like a boulder!

The four men looked up sharply. "We're being spied on!" one of them cried out.

Pete jumped to his feet. "Come on, Bunky! Run for it!" he yelled.

As they dashed off, the infuriated men raced after them. Murch, with the speed of a cougar, caught up to the boys and hurled himself at them.

All three tumbled to the stony ground in a tangle of arms and legs. Then Pete felt a huge hand grasp the back of his neck and jerk him to his feet.

"Who are you?" the broad-shouldered man demanded.

"I'll tell you!" Murch shouted. "They're the kids who stole our gold!"

CHAPTER 18

Renegade Roundup

THE gruff man shook Pete. "Where is the gold?" he rumbled.

"At the ranch," Pete said bravely. "And it doesn't belong to you, 'cause this is Mr. Blair's property!"

"And he's my father!" Bunky spoke up, trying to shake free of Murch's grasp.

"Oh, so you're young Blair!" the tall man said. "How nice. Maybe we could hold you for ransom."

"You better let us both go!" Pete declared stoutly. "The police are on your trail."

"The police we've managed to fool," Murch said with a sneer. "It's only you Hollisters who spoiled our plans."

Pete hoped fervently that Old Dad and the others had heard the scuffle and had retreated to get immediate help. In order to give them time to get away, Pete tried to stall by questioning his captors.

"Where's Dakota Dawson?" the boy asked. "He's working with you, isn't he?"

"Dawson?" the short, rotund man said. "Who's he?"

"You know well enough," Bunky continued.

"Enough of this gabble," Murch interrupted. He addressed the tall broad-shouldered man. "What'll we do with these spies, Rocky?"

"We'll tie 'em up," the big fellow replied, "after we catch the others who were riding with them."

Pete's heart sank. The gang knew all about their mountain trek! "Which one of you was following us?" he asked spunkily.

Murch laughed. "I was. You nearly caught me the night I prowled around your camp."

"Then you're the one who sent that rock slide down on us!" Pete declared hotly.

"It nearly got you, didn't it?" the wiry man answered. "I was watching you right along. I knocked over a boulder by accident."

"You should have done it on purpose," Rocky said with a snarl in his voice. He added, "Come on, let's get the others."

Dragging Pete and Bunky along with them, the four men marched toward the rocky passage which led out of the box canyon. On the way, Pete spied four horses picketed to one side of the antelope pen. One of them was the Appaloosa which belonged to Tut Primrose.

Pete held his breath as they approached the rocky cleft in the wall. Would Old Dad and the others be there? Would they too be caught by these ruffians?

When they reached the place no one was in sight. "If they got away, they can't be far," Rocky declared. He turned to the other two men. "Coyle! Minter!" he snapped. "Get your horses and chase them. It's an old man and kids. They can't go fast."

Just as the two henchmen started for their horses, a tall lean cowboy stepped out of the shadow of the cleft. "Halt, all of you!" he commanded.

The four men wheeled about in surprise.

"You're under arrest!" the cowboy called out.

"Dakota Dawson!" Pete cried.

"He's a law man!" Bunky shouted in relief.

"Stand away from those youngsters," Dakota ordered, striding forward.

But instead of obeying, the ruffians scattered into the brush like jack rabbits. Suddenly a rock flew from the bush concealing Murch. It hit Dakota in the side and he fell to the ground with a cry of pain.

Instantly the four men jumped from their hiding places and made a dash for their horses. Rocky and Coyle were in the lead, with Minter and Murch racing behind them.

Seeing what was happening, Pete and Bunky sprinted after and leaped on the backs of Murch and Minter, bringing them to the ground. The boys and their opponents struggled furiously until Dakota regained his feet. Then the tall, powerful cowboy collared the two men. Quickly he snapped handcuffs on each.

"The other two got away!" Pete cried.

"We're going after them," Dakota declared grimly.

As he spoke, Ricky and the girls ran out of the rocky cleft and joined them. Old Dad was limping behind.

"Where have you been?" Bunky asked.

"Dakota made us hide in a cranny in the vault," Gina replied.

"Picked up your trail in the pass this noon," Dakota explained as he whipped a rope from his belt. "Followed you here to the box canyon." Swiftly he tied the line around Murch's waist, talking as he worked.

"If it hadn't been for you young detectives I might never have found this hide-out." He smiled. "When I heard Pete and Bunky had gone for a closer look at these varmints, I figured there might be trouble, so I told the others to hide."

Now the cowboy quickly made a loop around Minter's waist, allowing several feet of rope between him and Murch.

"You certainly had us fooled," Pam said to Dakota.

Talking fast, Dakota told them that he was a sheriff's deputy and one of the Salt Creek Sheriff's Posse. Posing as a lonesome cowboy, he was dispatched secretly to work on the Tumbling K so that he could scour the Ruby Mountains for the source of the mysterious lights. "Police Chief Larney sent for me to do the job," Dakota added, "because he thought I was less likely to be recognized than an Elkton deputy."

"I'm so happy," Holly said, "that you aren't really a bad man."

"Mother was right after all," Ricky had to admit.

With a glance at the scowling prisoners, Dakota handed the end of their rope to Old Dad. "Somebody has to herd these two critters and the antelopes out of Rustlers' Canyon," he said, "while the boys and I go after the ones that got away."

"But watch out," Pete cautioned. "They may be tricky."

"Don't worry," Old Dad said with a wink at Dakota. "The girls will take my rope and fasten the baby animals to one another, and right at the head of the line we'll tie Mr. Murch and Mr. Minter. Then, no matter where they try to run to, on horseback or afoot, a dozen antelopes go with them!"

"Just what I had in mind," Dakota declared with a grin, and ran to the rocky cleft. "Wait at the mouth of the canyon," he called back. "We'll send a truck to pick you up there!" With that, he disappeared into the opening, the boys at his heels.

A few minutes later, when they swung into their saddles, Pete said, "I'll bet Rocky and Coyle headed down the canyon because that way they can get to the highway and maybe leave their horses and hitch a ride."

Dakota agreed, and they set off quickly. How proud the boys were as they rode behind the deputy!

At the mouth of the canyon Dakota turned in the saddle. "There's one question I can't answer yet," he said. "Where do these rascals keep that jeep they've been using to catch the antelopes?"

The four rode on in silence. While the others kept a sharp lookout for the renegades, Ricky pondered the question. He thought hard about his climb up to the cave where he had seen the mountain lion. He thought, too, of the scramble down the rocky slope, where he had picked up the splinters in his Levi's.

"And what," he asked himself, "were those two big eyes looking at me from the back of the cave? They really couldn't be those of a giant mountain lion."

The youngster spurred his horse and rode shoulder to shoulder with Dakota Dawson. He told him everything that had happened when first they had trailed the jeep of the antelope thieves.

"I have an idea," Ricky added.

"Let's hear it, son," the deputy answered.

"Well," Ricky said earnestly, "maybe those crooks had a couple of long planks hidden back in the cave. They could have carried them down and placed them so that they made a bridge from the back of Icy River to the rock slope."

"Go on," Dakota urged him.

"Then, when they drove the jeep to the water's edge, they only had to back it up the planks to the slope and on up into the cave. Afterwards," Ricky concluded, "they could drag the boards back to their hiding place."

"Crickets!" Pete declared. "The planks must have left splinters on the rough rock. That's how you got them in your breeches."

Now Dakota reined up his horse and looked Ricky directly in the eyes. "Boy," he said, "I think you've answered the question. Those big eyes you saw in the cave are probably the headlights of the missing jeep!"

Ricky sat proudly in his saddle. He grinned and scratched his red hair. "I should have thought of that long ago," he said.

"It's our fault 'cause we didn't believe you saw two big eyes in there," Pete declared.

"I'll bet that's where Rocky and Coyle are headed right now!" Bunky said excitedly. "They'll try to make a getaway in the jeep."

From there on the four rode rapidly until at last they reached the rocky slope and the cave. Dakota dismounted. He ordered the three boys into the shelter of a clump of trees, saying, "I hesitated to use my pistol in the box canyon when you children were in there. But if those

171

two men are hiding in the cave now, I'll have to flush them out."

The three boys quickly obeyed, and watched from a safe distance while Dakota, with long strides, climbed up the slope. Standing beside the cave mouth, he called out in a commanding voice, "All right, you in there, come out with your hands up!"

In a moment two men emerged from the shadows.

"Rocky and Coyle!" Pete exclaimed. "Now we've caught them all!"

"You were right, Ricky!" Dakota Dawson called down. "The jeep is in here, and the planks too!"

The deputy then led his handcuffed prisoners down the slope, and the boys emerged from the clump of trees, bringing the two horses the ruffians had hidden there.

Just then four men galloped up and quickly dismounted. They were Police Chief Larney and three of his men. "Terry Bridger told us the Tumbling K riders needed help," Larney said, striding up to Dakota Dawson. "I see you found them."

"Yes," the deputy smiled. "And *they* found the gang."

"Congratulations!" Larney said warmly. He glanced at the big prisoner. "Is this the ringleader of the mysterious prowlers?"

"Yes," Bunky replied. "Do you know him?"

"I sure do. That's Rocky Redmond. He was released from State prison only two months ago."

Then Dakota suggested that Larney's men take the jeep from the cave and go to meet Old Dad and the girls at the entrance to Rustlers' Canyon. The chief agreed.

"Now we've caught them all!"

"Two of you herd the prisoners to town, and one of you drive the antelopes down to the valley and turn them loose," he ordered, as the men started up the slope.

"You and I can head these two varmints for the hoosegow, Larney," Dakota added.

"And as soon as Old Dad and the girls catch up to us, we'd better head for home," Pete declared. "Crickets, I'm hungry!"

It was dark by the time the children and Old Dad finally sat down to a hot supper at the Tumbling K Ranch. The day had been long, and they were too weary to tell their whole story.

But the next morning at breakfast the children related every step of the startling adventure. As the two women, Mr. Blair, Sue, and Millie listened, Dakota Dawson came in quietly and joined them.

The cowboy said that the four prisoners had confessed everything in order to get lighter sentences.

"It all started," he went on, "when Rocky stumbled on a document telling about gold in the box canyon. With four of his cronies he invaded your land, Mr. Blair, and was conducting a thriving mining operation up there."

"And Murch was their messenger," Pam put in. "It was his job to pick up the gold and take it to the outside."

Dakota explained that, when Murch told the gang that Mr. Blair might sell his land to Mr. Simpson, they were afraid the new owner would discover them. Then Murch found out that Millie was timid, and the gang decided to display flickering lights to frighten her.

The child blushed when she heard this, and Pam squeezed her hand. "I'm really going to try not to be such a 'fraidy cat," Millie whispered.

"It was also Murch's job to harass Mr. Blair, Bunky, and Gina in New York," Dakota concluded, "so that the land deal wouldn't take place."

The cowboy rose. "And now," he said, "I want you all to come with me to Elkton. We need the children and Old Dad to identify the prisoners and give evidence."

An hour later the Hollisters and their friends were sitting in the prosecutor's office, as Pam finished her testimony. She looked across at the prisoners and added, "But we still don't know why they stole the antelopes."

"That was Murch's silly idea," Rocky said wrathfully. "He wanted to smuggle them out of the canyon later and sell them to roadside menageries."

"Well, he was a mean man to drop Prairie Star off the truck," Holly declared.

"I didn't do it!" Murch defended himself. "Rocky did that so you wouldn't follow us."

As the four men were led back to their cells, Rocky muttered, "You Hollisters have ruined my plans!"

"But they found a gold mine for our daddy," Gina said brightly.

"That's right," the rancher agreed happily. "Now I can afford to keep the Tumbling K."

That evening a celebration barbecue was held at the Tumbling K Ranch for everyone connected with the mystery.

As the sun was setting, Pete looked up at the mountains. "Isn't it funny," he said to Old Dad, "we solved the mystery without ever going to Secret Valley."

"And we never found the chest of gold," Ricky added regretfully.

"Boys," the white-haired cowboy replied, "the mountains will always have secrets. Just be proud you solved one of them."

When everyone had finished eating, Dakota Dawson and Mr. Blair rose and stood by the blazing fire.

The cowboy spoke first. "I want everybody to know that the Hollisters deserve full credit for solving the mystery," he announced warmly. "They did a wonderful job. They're real heroes." The children beamed modestly at the applause, and Sue clapped longer than anybody else.

Then Mr. Blair told them that as soon as he had mined enough of the precious metal he would reward each of the Hollister girls, including their mother, with a gold ring.

Everyone clapped again, and Old Dad hopped up. "For Pete and Ricky," he volunteered, "I promise to get a mountain-lion rug as soon as I can trap the varmint." Then his eyes twinkled and he added, "Unless Ricky wants to catch him himself."

Ricky grinned as everybody laughed. "No thanks!" he said fervently.

"We have a present for you, too, Ricky," Cindy announced as she and Millie stepped forward. "It's a part in the play. One of the boys had to drop out. We need somebody who can act very brave. And, after all, you're a real hero now."

"You'd be just wonderful in it," Millie said sincerely, holding out the play book to him.

"Would I?" Ricky asked, pleased.

"Of course you would!" Holly declared, and the other children echoed her.

"All right," he agreed, taking the book. "What do I have to do?"

"It's easy," Millie assured him. "Only three pages to learn, and you kiss the girl at the end."

Ricky turned scarlet to the roots of his hair.

"Kiss the girl!" he exclaimed. He pushed the book back into Millie's hands. "Kiss the girl!" the hero repeated. "Yikes! I'd rather kiss a mountain lion!"

Don't miss a single adventure –
collect all 33 volumes of
The Happy Hollisters by Jerry West!

1) The Happy Hollisters
2) The Happy Hollisters on a River Trip
3) The Happy Hollisters at Sea Gull Beach
4) The Happy Hollisters and the Indian Treasure
5) The Happy Hollisters at Mystery Mountain
6) The Happy Hollisters at Snowflake Camp
7) The Happy Hollisters and the Trading Post Mystery
8) The Happy Hollisters at Circus Island
9) The Happy Hollisters and the Secret Fort
10) The Happy Hollisters and the Merry-Go-Round Mystery
11) The Happy Hollisters at Pony Hill Farm
12) The Happy Hollisters and the Old Clipper Ship
13) The Happy Hollisters at Lizard Cove
14) The Happy Hollisters and the Scarecrow Mystery
15) The Happy Hollisters and the Mystery of the Totem Faces
16) The Happy Hollisters and the Ice Carnival Mystery
17) The Happy Hollisters and the Mystery in Skyscraper City
18) The Happy Hollisters and the Mystery of the Little Mermaid
19) The Happy Hollisters and the Mystery at Missile Town
20) The Happy Hollisters and the Cowboy Mystery
21) The Happy Hollisters and the Haunted House Mystery
22) The Happy Hollisters and the Secret of the Lucky Coins
23) The Happy Hollisters and the Castle Rock Mystery
24) The Happy Hollisters and the Cuckoo Clock Mystery
25) The Happy Hollisters and the Swiss Echo Mystery
26) The Happy Hollisters and the Sea Turtle Mystery
27) The Happy Hollisters and the Punch and Judy Mystery
28) The Happy Hollisters and the Whistle-Pig Mystery
29) The Happy Hollisters and the Ghost Horse Mystery
30) The Happy Hollisters and the Mystery of the Golden Witch
31) The Happy Hollisters and the Mystery of the Mexican Idol
32) The Happy Hollisters and the Monster Mystery
33) The Happy Hollisters and the Mystery of the Midnight Trolls

For more information about *The Happy Hollisters*,
visit www.TheHappyHollisters.com

Made in the USA
Middletown, DE
06 January 2023

21521594R00099